U0922947

第五期

SINO-AMERICAN JOURNAL *Of* COMPARATIVE LITERATURE

中美比较文学

主编　张　华
Paul Allen Miller

中国社会科学出版社

图书在版编目（CIP）数据

中美比较文学．第五期／张华，（美）保罗（Paul Allen Miller）主编．—北京：中国社会科学出版社，2021.9

ISBN 978-7-5203-8882-5

Ⅰ.①中… Ⅱ.①张… ②保… Ⅲ.①比较文学—文学研究—中国、美国 Ⅳ.①I206 ②I712.06

中国版本图书馆CIP数据核字（2021）第179188号

出 版 人 赵剑英
责任编辑 夏 侠
责任校对 陈 娟
责任印制 张雪娇

出 版 中国社会科学出版社
社 址 北京鼓楼西大街甲158号
邮 编 100720
网 址 http://www.csspw.cn
发 行 部 010-84083685
门 市 部 010-84029450
经 销 新华书店及其他书店

印 刷 北京君升印刷有限公司
装 订 廊坊市广阳区广增装订厂
版 次 2021年9月第1版
印 次 2021年9月第1次印刷

开 本 710×1000 1/16
印 张 9.5
插 页 2
字 数 138千字
定 价 68.00元

《中美比较文学》(*Sino-American Journal of Comparative Literature*)为北京语言大学创办，并由比较文学界同仁共同编辑的连续性出版物。中外学者的来稿由编委会负责审阅，该连续性出版物由中国社会科学出版社出版，中英文双语发行。

该连续性出版物旨在集中展示比较文学界在比较文学与世界文学学科范围内及相关学科的最新研究成果，探讨前沿理论问题，拓展文学批评空间，研究学术焦点现象，以促进比较文学与世界文学研究领域的最平等、最直接、最充分的学术交流。

Sino-American Journal of Comparative Literature is founded by Beijing Language and Culture University. The journal is published by the China Social Sciences Press both in English and in Chinese. The founder and editors, as well as the members of the editorial board, as experts in the field of comparative literature are responsible for refereeing all submissions. Articles submitted in Chinese and in English are edited by the editorial board.

The joumal is designed to be a platform to gather and exhibit the latest research findings in Comparative Literature, World Literature and related disciplines. Its mission is to explore the latest theoretical issues in both countries and to expand the range of literary criticism available in each. It aims to promote a full and critical dialogue in the field of Comparative Literature and World Literature as well as intercultural comprehension.

MILLER, Paul Allen (University of South Carolina)
RAPAPORT, Herman (Wake Forest University)
SHANKMAN, Steven (University of Oregon)
ZALLOUA, Zahi (Whitman College)

目 录

Introduction to the Fifth Issue

ZHANG Hua [*]

In the Internet era, watching movies is much more convenient, the quantity has changed greatly compared with the past, and the quality change can also be measured by data. It can be watched in the home theater, and the privacy is greatly enhanced; it can also be viewed in the public cinema to achieve the effect that is difficult to achieve in the home cinema; some films that we wanted to see but could not see in the past are now readily available.

Wu Tianming, a famous director, has a very important and special position in the history of Chinese film and even in the history of world film, and is an indispensable and irreplaceable figure in the fourth generation of directors. After Wu Tianming's death in 2014, a series of commemorative articles were published in the domestic media, and later a commemorative collection was published, but relatively few academic research papers were published. Among foreign academic circles, the scholars from University of South Carolina in the United States began to study Wu Tianming earlier, with a variety of perspectives and rich viewpoints, which stems from the fact that the University of South Carolina has the richest and most complete

* 作者为北京语言大学比较文学与世界文学专业教授，博士生导师，《中美比较文学》集刊中方主编。

Chinese theme film materials in the world, and has a strong and complete teaching and research team, Professor YE Tan is the team leader. The five English papers included in this issue of *Sino-American Journal of Comparative Literature* are all from this university, four of which are about Chinese film studies.

Speaking of Chinese film studies, I ever gave several keynote speeches at the Annual International Forum on Chinese Cinema held by the University of South Carolina, one of them in 2012 entitled *How to Understand Chinese Films Today?* I would like to take this opportunity to put part of it here.

> If you ever read about Luxun, one of the greatest modern writers and poets in 1930s, you probably know one of his famous essays titled *How should we be a father today?* (《今天我们如何做父亲？》) I give my paper's title How do we understand Chinese Films Today from his essay's inspiration. This title in Chinese, it is"今天我们如何看中国电影？"(Jintian Women Ruhe Kan Dianying ?) This 看（kan）has two meanings, one is 观看，means " to watch", another is 看待，means "to look on", "to understand". Although in English, I used "understand", when I talk about " How to", I still take care of both meanings.

Actually, it is no exaggeration to say that in the"theoretical circles"or academia of today's China, few people know the original meaning of "theory" (Theorein, Theoria, "watching""contemplation") let alone its historical evolution. Anyway, I will not talk about the original meaning of "theory" which is also"watching"like Chinese 看（kan）. Nevertheless, how to watch film（如何看电影？ Ruhe Kan Dianying ?）should not be a question. You only need to sit there, you may stand or lie there if you prefer, and watch. Then, since 100 readers can get 100 Hamlets, everybody can have their own understanding or interpretation about what they have watched. But, a question always is raised by others after their watching. That is 看懂

了吗（Kandong le ma）, that means: Did you fully understand the film you just watching? Or, sometimes it becomes a very common comment or direct answer even nobody asks the question after watching, 我没看懂。这电影想说明什么？(Wo Mei Kandong. Zhe Dianying Xiang Shuoming Shenme? I could not understand, what does the film tell us?) This phenomenon, in some sense, has become a reading custom of Chinese readers or watching custom of Chinese audience. In other words, it has become part of Chinese film culture.

From my understanding, it may not be correct, I generally classify world film into two sorts or categories, one is artistic film, like the European countries especially France always made; another sort is entertainment film, like the Hollywood always making. Of course, I am saying this doesn't mean artistic film does not have entertainment, and vice versa. But, if you take a look at Chinese films today, you'll find it is quite difficult to put all the films of today's China into those two categories.

I myself classify Chinese films in a way that "whether it is easy to be understood", then the first level should be the films which are easiest in understanding— 主旋律电影 (main theme films), for instance, 五个一工程电影 (Five One Project Film①). Those kind of films are moving, even kids are tearing when they are watching. It is never difficult to be understood. Sometimes it has artistic consideration, and most are paying more attention on political ideology; Second level, easier in understanding— 贺岁片 (New Year's Film), film makers of this kind of films pursue or seek a joint of entertainment with artistic, but they have to express a main theme which can be accept, because of this, it often made the film like the first sort; Third level, difficult in understanding—including artistic films like what JIA Zhangke made, even anthropological films. Some people call it ethnographical films.

---

① Five One Project means one good book, one good TV series, one good play, one good film, and one good article.

When you mentioned about artistic films, a lot of people will think they are obscure. Even *the Red Sorghum*, one of the earlier works of MO Yan, the Nobel Prize winner in literature, made by ZHANG Yimou. When it was first screening 30 years ago, most the audience said it was difficult to be understood. The *Red Sorghum* directed by ZHANG Yimou, as the first Chinese film representative won an international award at that moment. Lots of people think that is because this film shows Chinese people have no culture, exposes the badly-rooted Chinese habit. Somebody even said the reason it won the prizes because it tells the world that Chinese also have wild nature, also can make love in the red sorghum field…Even *the Brokeback* and *Lust, Caution* made by LI An（Ang Lee）, I found many people said they were not able to understand, and keep on asking what LI An wants to tell us. They said in *the Brokeback* they only got the homosexuality and in *Lust, Caution* they take it as 三级片（X-rated film）.

Talking about the anthropological films or Ethnographical films, I would like to introduce a very close friend, John Paul Sniadecki. He likes people call him J. P. or 史杰鹏 (SHI Jiepeng). I organized for him several film screenings at BLCU, which including《松花》(Songhua)《拆、迁》(Chai, Qian) and《四川记事》(Sichuan Jishi), *New York Parts*, etc. He got many award in France, Germany and Denmark by his works, but when these films were screening in BLCU, many many people commented that why this kind of films can get international awards? The audience keep on ask these kind of questions is because they may not fully understand these kind of films. So these kind of films only can find their bosom friends in some certain circles.

Actually, in my attitude, we got used to the meta-narratives, got used to listen to others telling us stories. When we were kids, we listened to our parents; when we were teenagers, we listened to our teachers, when we got a job, we still have to listen to others telling stories.

Today, there is a saying quite popular, which is "学会讲好中国故

事 "—that means "learning to tell Chinese stories well". I think, before we telling a Chinese story to other countries, we need to understand ourselves well, that apparently includes understanding Chinese films. I know I did not give a answer to the question on the title, only raised this question, but you know it is very important to think independently and will have your own answer about that.

Another English article in this issue, not about film, but about education, is written by Daria SMIRNOVA from Russia, who is currently studying for a doctorate in comparative literature at the University of South Carolina in the United States. This article is her speech at the 21st Annual Conference of Comparative Literature in South Carolina (Borders and Borderlands in the Age of Globalization, March 29–30, 2019, USC.)

The themes of the three Chinese articles are also very distinct, all of which are related to Sino-American literary exchanges and Qiao-Yiology, to be more precise, the three articles have interpreted and studied a key academic project achievement of China, *The History of Sino-Foreign Literary Exchange*, from the perspective or angle of Qiao-Yiology, and the focus of the three articles is on Sino-American volumes.

In recent years, more and more people have learned about the study of Qiao-Yiology in China's domestic academic circles, and in the international arena, German scholars who pay attention to Sinology and Chinese studies have also learned about it. It is an academic method or interpretation perspective initiated by Professor YE Jun. In other words, Qiao-Yiology is a term that can best represent and reflect Professor YE Jun's academic achievements. YE Jun is currently a professor of Humanities College of Tongji University and a doctoral supervisor of cultural history and philosophy. He has done research in academic institutions in Britain, France and Germany. Monographs include *Bian-Chuang and Jian-Chang—the idea of Qiao-Yiology* (《变创与渐常——侨易学的观念》), *A Theoretical Introduction to the Germanology* (《德国学理论初探》), *The Game*

Playing of the Different Cultures (《异文化博弈》), *The Transformation of the Subject* (《主体的迁变》), *The Other Western Learning* (《另一种西学》), *The Making of Goethe's Thoughts* (《歌德思想之形成》), *Study on the Academic History of Johann Wolfgang von Goethe* (《歌德学术史研究》) and so on; The collection of academic essays includes *the Spiritual Criterion of the University* (《大学的精神尺度》), *The Spiritual Trouble of the Epoch—Essays on the German-speaking Literature* (《时代的精神忧患：德语文学论集》), *Essays on the Sino-German Cultural Relationships* (《中德文化关系评论集》) and so on; Professor YE is also chief editor of *Sino-German Culture Series* (《中德文化丛书》), *Academic Studies in the Republic of China Series* (《民国学术丛刊》), *History of Study Abroad Series* (《留学史丛书》) and so on; He translated *Education and the Future* (《教育与未来》) with others as well. His academic interests now focus on German classical literature, intellectual history and Qiao-Yiology.

The magazine *Beautiful Prose* (Meiwen,《美文》) edited by the famous Chinese writer JIA Pingwa, once published an essay entitled "Cherishing the Memory of Grandparents" written by YE Jun. At the end of the essay, YE Jun wrote: "Every individual can't avoid the fate of struggling in the great era. Grandfather is like this, and so is grandmother. Their life course is insignificant, and it seems so insignificant against the background of the great era. I often wonder, without my records and thinking, whether their life history is bound to be like a lonely leaf withering in autumn, coming and going alone, leaving no trace of stars in the great history? But when I heard such an elaboration of life history, I was moved, not only as an individual's sympathy and sadness, but also as a historian's consciousness and touch."

Out of the academic understanding of Professor YE Jun, when I read here, I feel that this prose in memory of my grandparents is the extension of his academic thinking of studying and writing history, from the celebrities and masters in the traditional academic history, ideological history and life history to the unknown generation, and then to the most ordinary life individual. From grand narrative, major achievements, great course to ordinary and universal feelings, mental journey and even details of life.

The basic idea of Qiao-Yiology is Yi caused by Qiao. The former emphasizes the integration of space dimension, while the latter focuses on the evolution of time dimension, which includes not only the formation and creation of individual ideas caused by material displacement and spiritual roaming, but also the interaction and spiritual deformation of different cultural subsystems. Popularly speaking, it is to grasp the changeable law of the spiritual level by carefully observing the material or physical migration or displacement of the object of study. Qiao comes from LI Shizeng's *Outline of Qiao*(Qiaoxue Fafan,《侨学发凡》) and Yi comes from *the Book of Changes* (《易经》). This also constitutes YE Jun's two theoretical bases for putting forward the Qiao-Yiology. YE Jun hopes to excavate the rich resources of Qiao-Yiology, establish the research object, core content and basic principles of Qiao-Yiology, and on this basis, apply this approach to analyze a large number of cases in academic history to verify and improve this theory.

Apparently, this world is a world of moving and changing both physically and spiritually. The Humboldt Forum has set up a sub-forum on Qiao-Yiology for many times, and it was set up again in 2020. Scholars from different countries and different humanities disciplines once again exchanged on Qiao-Yiology. This also fully shows that Qiao-Yiology is an interdisciplinary and cross-cultural academic perspective, approach and vision, and after its theoretical system is perfected, there will be different disciplines of Qiao-Yiology, such as Qiao-Yiology of literature, Qiao-Yiology of philosophy and Qiao-Yiology of history. I am very much looking forward to this and full of confidence for this.

Hollywood and the Chinese Cinema

YE Tan *

中文摘要 本文分五个历史阶段论述了自19世纪末中国第一篇影评发表以来中美电影之间的交流与互动。在经典好莱坞时期，中国只是异国情调的艺术来源地，并非其潜在的目标市场。随着好莱坞影业发展成熟，进入黄金期后，数量空前的好莱坞影片涌入中国，但中国本土电影自有其文化特征，并未受到好莱坞的影响。新中国成立后，好莱坞影片一度被禁止在中国放映，中间一些20世纪30–40年代的好莱坞经典虽有上映，也仅被当作批评斗争的对象。直到中国改革开放后，好莱坞电影重返中国市场，受到了中国第四代电影人和普通观影者的追捧。自20世纪80年代末90年代初，中国艺术和文化进入多元化发展阶段，第五代电影人也逐渐摸索出中国电影发展的新道路。

关键词 电影；好莱坞；中国；时代

In the post-colonial era, Hollywood films have often been treated by scholars on both sides of the Pacific as a form of cultural invasion; and

* 作者为美国南卡罗莱纳大学比较文学专业终身教授，主要研究领域为比较戏剧和电影研究。

China, the reluctant victim of this invasion. My discursive review of the interaction between Hollywood and the Chinese Cinema is intended not to negate the invasion-and-resistance theory in general but to repute the generalization of the "Chineseness" in the cultural exchanges of more than two centuries. In China, there has never been a uniform opinion of Hollywood, because there has never been a single, faceless entity of the Chinese. In China, authorities' opinions, art elites' opinions, filmmakers' opinions, cineastes' opinions, and masses' opinions have always differed, sometimes polarized, from one another. Two perspectives, to treat Hollywood as a political entity and to treat it as a provider of entertainment, have been the major demarcation of the differences. Any failure to differentiate these opinions is a failure to understand the complexity of the Chinese mentality and history. In this essay, the term, "Hollywood" is used to distinguish commercial ventures from auteur films, independent films, or underground films made in the United States, and "audience" is referred to the average cinema goers who view films, not just Hollywood films, as a sheer means of entertainment.

Historically, the relationship between Hollywood and China can be divided into five phases. The first phase (1895–1927) covers the Classical Hollywood period. The second phase (1927–1949) starts with Hollywood's Golden Years and ends shortly after the establishment of the People's Republic of China. The third phase (1949–1979) embraces the thirty years of Maoist control, when Hollywood was banned in China. The fourth phase (1979–1989) begins with the reintroduction of Hollywood to China and ends with the Tiananmen Square Incident. The last phase (1989–present) is the Post Deng Era, from Tiananmen to the present.

I. The Inspiration: Introducing American Films to China: 1895–1927

China was among the few countries exposed to cinematic culture at a very early stage. A year after he invented cinematography in France, Louis Lumeire sent his cameraman to Shanghai to show some shots (it was not yet a film in the modern sense) of magic and acrobatic performances. The historical date was August 11, 1896. Another year had barely passed, when James Rication, an American from Maplewood, NJ, arrived in China to exhibit some episodes shot in America. In those early episodes, the principle of Hollywood had already emerged: to entertain with novelty and sensuality. In 1897, the first film review in Chinese history was published in Shanghai. It refers to Rication's show as an "American electrical light shadow play" and the word "shadow" is typically Daoist:

> American electrical light shadow play... magical and illusionary, all beyond imagination.... Two fluffy-haired blondes dance in a charmingly naive manner... Two Westerners wrestle.... Two Russian princesses dance to music... A woman bathing... Bothered by a bedbug, a guy tries to catch it... A magician covers a female with a blanket. When he lifts the blanket, she has disappeared.... All these tricks cannot be comprehended.... The strangest scene is a bicycle race... I then heave a deep sigh: thousands of changes between heaven and earth... are similar to what we see in the shadow play.... Life is nothing but shadow of bubbles. ①

---

① "Watching American Electrical Light Shadow Play," *Youxibao* (*Play Journal*), No. 74. September 5, 1897. Throughout the essay, all the Chinese-English translation and emphases are mine.

"Dianying (electrical shadow)," the Chinese term for "film," is perhaps derived from the above review. The first Chinese to enter this growing "electrical shadow" business was Lin Chushan, who in 1903 brought back from America a projector and rented a teahouse in Beijing's theater district to show some episodes shot in the U. S. So, the first film shown by a Chinese to a Chinese audience was American. At that time, this film was not accessible in most parts of the US, which in 1905 had only ten cinemas nationwide. Contrary to what many people would assume, the court of the Qing dynasty was not against this dazzling innovation from the West. In 1904, a British official presented a film at the Empress Dowager's palace in Beijing. It was a disaster, which resulted not from the content of the film but from an electrical fire caused by a primitive generator. Even so, Her Majesty only banned the film inside her palace, not outside.

The period of Classical Hollywood is usually dated between 1906 and 1927. The Chinese film industry came into being almost simultaneously. Between 1905 and 1908, Fengtai Photography Shop in Beijing made its first film, "Dingjun Mountain". Shot with a French camera and film cassettes bought from a German photography supply store in Beijing, it was a Beijing Opera adopted from a popular Chinese novel, *The Three Kingdoms*. General Huang Zhong, the hero of the film, was played by Tan Xinpei, an eminent Beijing Opera performer patronized by the Empress Dowager. This film was a classic application of a doctrine prevalent in the last years of the Qing dynasty: "[to treat] Chinese learning as the foundation and Western learning as utilities." It was eight years prior to the establishment of Hollywood. At the turn of the century, American films did not have any superiority in China, where most foreign films were imported from France. At that time, English and German films were also quite popular. Although China's first counter with the West was characterized with distrust and resistance, the advent of film was never resisted by the Chinese audience. Within one decade, cinemas were established in all major Chinese cities. In June 1911, the Qing court issued "Regulations of Film Plays" in Shanghai, forbidding "showing films without a license," "films containing obscenity," "male and female viewers sitting together," and "showing films after mid-night."① Considering the traditional moral concerns and stern control over art and literature in feudal China, these earliest restrictions on films were not exceptionally harsh and they were not specially targeted at American films.

Exactly a half century later, *The Chinese History of Film Development*, which was then the most authoritative, summarizes this period with the following words:

> Due to the lengthy stagnation of Chinese feudalism, especially to its semi-colonial and semi-feudal condition caused by imperialist invasions, Chinese science and technology was extremely backward. Therefore, Chinese cinema started with films made not by Chinese but by foreigners. [The birth of] Chinese cinema was a result of imperial commercial export and cultural invasion. Although it was not yet an established art form, film was already opium of the decadence from imperialist "civilization." Nevertheless, the appearance of films in China did bring a new form of entertainment to Chinese people and was welcomed by the [Chinese] audience. It also aroused some intellectuals' desire to make Chinese films.②

Reading it today, we may feel that the above summary is politicized, but given the situation in the 1960s, when all Western films were banned in China and Sino-Western cultural exchanges had been withheld for more than a decade, it took some courage for the authors to reveal the truth that

① Li Shaobai, "Historical Background of Chinese Film Development" ("Zhongguo dianying fasheng de lishi wenhua beijing"), *Yingshi wunhua* (*Film and TV Culture*), Vol. 4: 68.

② Cheng Jihua, et al. *Zhongguo dianying fazhanshi* (*The Chinese History of Film Development*). Beijing: Chinese Film Press, 1962: 13.

the first Western films introduced to China were entertaining, and both common audience and intellectuals welcomed them. As a result, when the Cultural Revolution broke out in 1966, all the copies of *The Chinese History of Film Development* were burned and all of its three authors persecuted for "distorting history" and "rampantly attacking Mao Zedong's guidelines for art and literature."①

By 1909, there were already more than 10,000 cinemas in the United States. About ten years after the First World War, Hollywood became the superpower of the film world. Supported by a peaceful domestic environment and rapid economic growth, a group of talented individuals started to shape an effective system of film production in America and to win fame all over the world. Like the atmospheric "Oriental," theaters constructed in America in the 1920s, oriental images created by Hollywood were stereotyped but not always, as some film historians assert, negative. In spite of its obvious commercial purposes, which were devoid of any genuine interest in comprehending the "inscrutable," Hollywood never formed a unified perception for, or against, Chinese. The 16–part "The Yellow Menace" produced in 1916 is undoubtedly a shining example of a racist attitude against Asians. But "Broken Blossoms", which has often been used to exemplify the distorted image of Chinese people, is not exactly the case. Directed by D. W. Griffith in 1919, it depicts a sensitive Chinese man who saves a white girl abused by her father. Consequently, he is murdered by her father, the villain in the tale. The Chinese man appears mystic and feminine but not at all evil. His admiration for the girl is spiritual and his caring for her, unselfish. As claimed in the prologue of the film, "Broken Blossoms" advocates such Confucian virtues as "gentleness and benevolence." These two films are better understood in their historical contexts. "The Yellow Menace" is a reenactment of the age-

① Chen Huangmei, "Republication Preface" to *Zhongguo dianying fazhanshi*. Beijing: Chinese Film Press, 1981: 2–3.

long nightmare caused by the Mongolian invasion of Europe; whereas "Broken Blossoms" serves as a contemporary reminder of the fragility of China in the face of Western invasions at the turn of the century. In this period, two other controversial films about the Chinese were produced, "The Mask of Fu Manchu" and "The Bitter Tea of General Yen". While the former creates a prototype of the wise and wicked detective who functions well in a dramatic situation but reveals little complexity in characterization; the latter presents a much more complicated warlord who is at the same time a pervert and a gallant.

During the silent film era, most Chinese filmmakers were from drama circle, whose film training was minimal. Like their counterparts in Japan, Chinese filmmakers' education was a combination of oldfashioned apprenticeship in the studio and observation of Hollywood products. Thematically, Hollywood did not exert any significant influence on the Chinese film industry. Technologically, however, China learned a great deal from America. Practical skills such as analytical editing, soft focus, backlighting, masking (blocking off parts of the frame image to create different shapes within the frame) and so on were all borrowed from Hollywood.

During the first phase, Hollywood treated China as a source of exoticism to attract its domestic audience rather than a potential market in international competition. There is no record that any of those films was shown in China.

Once Hollywood was ready to conquer the world, the first country its eyes turned to was China. For a time, American filmmakers seriously contemplated taking advantage of China's cheap labor and material as well as its exotic scenery. The first joint venture, American Oriental Picture Company, was established in 1926. "Shattered Jade Fated to be ReUnited", the first Chinese film made with American money, was a melodrama derived from the Chinese classical theater—a promising beginning. Had the First Civil War not broken out in China and thus made further investment infeasible, making film in China could have become very profitable for Hollywood. Because of the war, Hollywood gave up the idea of producing films in China; instead it doubled its efforts to export films to this country, whose own film industry was seriously crippled by the war.

II. The Dominance: Hollywood Golden Years in China: 1927–1949

The year 1927 was significant for Hollywood and China in different ways. For Hollywood, it was the beginning of its golden age. For China, it was the first serious clash between the Nationalists and Communists, a clash that was to split the country for the rest of the century. While the Chinese were busy making wars against each other, Hollywood was busy making films for the world, including China. Before long, Hollywood dominated the global market. The average percentage of Hollywood films on the international market was 75% and in China was between 85% and 90%. In 1936, for example, China imported 367 foreign films, of which 328 were made by Hollywood.

The transition from silent to sound film was completed. While old comedians like Chaplin could still cheer Chinese up, new tragediennes like Greta Garbo had already begun to soften Chinese hearts. Rather than hampering the advance of Hollywood, the Depression boosted it, driving millions to cinemas to temporarily forget their worries. During this phase Hollywood gained the name of "dream factory." Escapism—some modern puritans may also call it "plebeianism"—served its purpose, both for Americans during the Depression and for Chinese during the war. If, in the previous phase, China was Hollywood's source of exoticism, now, watching American Westerns, musicals, gangster films, screwball comedies and science fictions, it was the Chinese people who enjoyed exoticism from America. Learning more technique from Hollywood, the First Generation① of Chinese filmmakers' format became standardized as Hollywood's. Usually a film would start with a panoramic view that was followed by a long shot, a medium shot, and finally a close-up. Straight angle, 3-point lighting (key, back, fill-in), and simple dialogue were the mainstream.

When the War of Resistance against Japan broke out in 1937, Hollywood produced one of its most pro-China films, "Good Earth". Directed by Sidney Franklin, the film faithfully rendered Pearl Buck's Nobel winning novel. Set in premodern China, the film transformed the vicissitudes of an ordinary woman into a saga of all the Chinese peasantry. Wang Long, the hero played by Paul Muni, is a simple farmer who works hard to become a prosperous landlord. Tragedy follows along the way as he betrays his family and neglects the earth he has worshiped. Nonetheless, the real Good Earth is embodied by his wife, a meek yet obdurate servant girl played by Luise Rainer. From a battered slave the girl grows into a proud, noble lady whose spirit represents the indomitable strength of the Chinese in the face of danger and misfortune. Rainer's convincing portrayal of the Chinese woman won her the title of the Best Actress of that year's Oscar.

Hollywood's golden years were also its most successful years in China. Never did Hollywood show more films in China: "The Wizard of Oz", "Mr. Smith Goes to Washington", "Only Angels Have Wings", and "Stagecoach"—to name just a few. By the end of this phase, more than 4,000 Hollywood films had been shown in China. The War of Resistance against Japan and the Chinese Civil War gave birth to the Second Generation of Chinese filmmakers. During and after the war, the Second Generation, like the rest of the nation, regarded America as a reliable friend and teacher.

---

① Until now the division of the generations of Chinese film directors is still not finalized, the following is a compromise of several contradicting but influential opinions: The First Generation (1905–1937); The Second Generation (1937–1949); The Third Generation (1949–1978); The Fourth Generation (1978–1983); The Fifth Generation (1983–1989); The Sixth Generation (1989–1996) .

Knowledgeable not only on American films but also on Western literature, this generation were particularly fond of such influential Hollywood adaptations of literature as *Gone with the Wind* and *Wuthering Heights*. After musicals by Cole Porter, Irving Berlin, Jerome Kern, and George Gershwin took China by storm, the Second Generation began to make their own musicals. Most of their attempts were mediocre, including the relatively successful "Ten Thousand Violets and One Thousand Red Blossoms" ("Wanzi qianhong"), whose borrowing of Micky Mouse, Bunny girls, candles and birthday cakes appeared awkward in the Chinese cultural context. The more successful films produced by the Second Generation were realistic ones that dealt with contemporary life and war in China. If films like "Street Angel" ("Malu tianshu") directed by Yuan Muzhi and *Crossroads* (*Shizi jietou*) by Shen Xiling bore some resemblance to American realistic acting and miseenscene but no evidence of intentional learning from Hollywood, Xia Yan's comedy, "Money Tree" ("Yaoqian shu"), clearly used Sean O'Casey's "Juno and the Paycock" as its model. Hollywood influence was also obvious in "Small Toy" ("Xiao wanyi") and other films directed by Sun Yu, who had been trained in America.

Unlike their French or Italian counterparts, Chinese filmmakers made no effort to avoid thematic repetition of Hollywood. They did not have to. The situation in China simply did not allow Chinese filmmakers to make stories similar to Hollywood films. The example of "Ten Thousand Violets and One Thousand Red Blossoms" was not followed simply because it was not appreciated by the majority of the Chinese audience and therefore not economically profitable. Through trial and error, the Chinese filmmakers drew inspiration more consciously from their own cultural tradition. In spite of budgetary problems, Chinese films like "Burning of Red Lotus Temple" ("Huoshao honglianshi", a glorification of martial art produced by Bright Star Studio in Shanghai) were successful enough to compete with Hollywood films.

For all their commercial concerns, the relationship between Hollywood and China has also been political in the sense that it has always been subordinate to the relationship between the two governments. As China's ally during the Second World War, America's general attitude toward the Chinese was the most sympathetic and Hollywood's general attitude was no exception. A conspicuous example is "The Battle of China" (1944), a documentary financed by the American Army and directed by Frank Capra, whose "The Bitter Tea of General Yen" is often cited as a sample of Hollywood's hostility toward the Chinese. "The Battle of China" exalts the pacifism of China to such an extent that it declares that although the Chinese invented gunpowder many centuries ago, they used it only as fireworks on festive occasions but never as ammunition in wars.

III. The Communication Stagnation: 1949–1979

With the absence of diplomatic relation between the US and PRC, Chinese filmmakers and the general public had no access to Hollywood films made in the 1950s and 1960s. During the first half of this phase most of the foreign films in China were imported from the Soviet Union and many Chinese filmmakers were trained in the Soviet Union. After China and the Soviet Union parted company, the foreign films publicly shown were made either in North Korea or in Albania. However, even in this isolation, under the excuse of "internal criticism", film professionals, students of cinema studies and English, and government officials could still screen some Hollywood films made in the 1930s and 1940s. Toward the end of the Cultural Revolution, more and more Hollywood classics were "internally criticized". Among them were "Rebecca", "Gone with the Wind", "My Fair Lady", "Singing in the Rain", and "The Sound of Music".

IV. The Idolization: 1979–1989

When the Fourth Generation began to make films, Hollywood came back to China. It was a time of confusion and hope. Old faith was vanishing rapidly; new faith was yet to be established. There was a huge void to be filled up and Hollywood was welcomed with exceptional enthusiasm. This time, the learning from Hollywood and from the West in general was systematic. Most of the important Western books on cinema and film criticism were introduced and discussed. The nationwide debate on the reformation of film language started in 1979 indicated serious efforts to break away from the Soviet format of filmmaking and to look for new alternatives.

At that time the Fifth Generation of filmmakers were still first year students at Beijing Film Academy. According to Li Tuo, a theorist who started the 1979 debate, the Fifth Generation was the first generation that studied Hollywood thoroughly[①]. They were allowed and encouraged to watch all the Hollywood classics in the National Film Archive. It was in this period that contemporary Hollywood films became available to the general public in China through both legal and illegal channels.

American films were shut out of China at a time when Hollywood suffered repeatedly from domestic box office failures. They were reintroduced to China soon after Hollywood recovered from its lean years. So, many Chinese, unaware that Hollywood had also come through a difficult period, regarded Hollywood as an unfailing film giant. New masterpieces like "Patton", "On Golden Pond", "Kramer vs. Kramer", and "Dear Hunter" were received with unqualified admiration. Numerous reviews and essays treated these films as typical examples of Hollywood and urged Chinese filmmakers

---

① My interview with Li Tuo on January 3, 1996.

to learn from them. So they did. Films like "Small Flower" ("Xiaohua") and "Laughter of a Bothered Man" ("Kunaoren de xiao") reveal apparent efforts to use Western film language either to enhance the narrative or to increase the complexity of characterization.

The halo of Hollywood began to diminish around the mid-1980s when the Fifth Generation began to claim their share at international film festivals. Several factors contributed to the decline of Hollywood superiority in China. First, by then Chinese filmmakers had seen enough Hollywood films, including some poorly made ones. Second, many talented directors from Japan, France, Italy, and other countries had been introduced to China. Third, after studying the history of Hollywood and that of Chinese cinema, Chinese filmmakers as well as film critics renewed the old faith that to make respectable Chinese films they needed to look into their own heritage. And finally, post-colonial theory and nationalism prompted Chinese filmmakers to challenge the superpower of Hollywood. The last factor becomes more noticeable in the next phase.

V. The Diversification: 1989–Present

As Zhang Yimou, the Fifth Generation have been able to view most recent foreign films and they have learned to avoid sensitive topics and to express their thoughts under such disguise as historical stories[①].

During the last decade, partially as a result of the rapid economic growth, Chinese people experienced a drastic diversification of ideas and attitudes. Film professionals now tend to view Hollywood with more skepticism, because, besides reasons mentioned previously in this essay, most

---

① My interview with Zhang Yimou on January 2, 1998. For details see "From 5th Generation to 6th Generation," *Film Quarterly*, University of California Press (Berkeley), Vol. 53, No. 2 Fall 99.

of them become more defensive to the arrogance of American (including Chinese American) critics who, although know little about the history of the Chinese cinema, constantly attribute the Fifth Generation's success to the patronage of Hollywood. The following is not uncommon of reviews written in America:

> Though in many ways an admirable filmmaker, he [Zhang Yimou] is doomed to be a cinephile's curiosity, notable primarily for a style that harks back without embarrassment to Fifties Hollywood. ①

Now more conscious of their own identity and cultural heritage, the Fifth Generation filmmakers find this kind of remarks offensive. When studying as a visiting artist in Cinema Studies at New York University, Chen Kaige was asked if he planned to make films in and about America. "I'm a Chinese filmmaker," Chen answered tersely, "I want to make films in and about China."② This of course does not suggest that Chen was ungrateful for the chance to study American films in America. Before returning to China, he told me that he had been like a fish that used to be confined to a small pond but after his study at NYU, he felt that he entered a big lake that enabled him to swim with big fish (i. e., established directors from the US and other countries)③.

On one hand, Chinese filmmakers think that international film festivals, particularly American ones, have not received them fairly; on the other hand, they feel that domestic politics in China has weakened their creative power to compete efficiently with film superpowers like Hollywood. The Fifth Generation's desire to win international awards is therefore at once a

---

① Stuart Klawans, "Zhang Yimou: Local Hero," *Film Comment*, Sep-Oct 1995: 13.

② Bernice Reynaud, "Distant Mirror: the Cinema of Chen Kaige," *The Independent*, Oct 1992: 28.

③ My conversation with Chen Kaige in the summer of 1980.

determination to prove themselves in the global film community and to defy the political pressure in China. When Zhang Yimou's "To Live" succeeded at a film festival, he expressed his delight in a tone of resentment.

> I am happy for Gong Li [the female lead in "To Live"] and Ge You [the male lead], not simply because they both received awards for their performances in my film. What makes me feel more excited is that their awards prove that European and American gentility have started acknowledging our performers. While appreciating Chinese films, they no longer focus on superficial oriental exoticism; instead they are now able to pay attention to our performers' portrayal of the characters. They do not keep pursuing Chinese films with a noveltyhunting mentality anymore but compare them [with films made in other countries] from the perspective of the human race. I hope Chinese performers will keep winning awards. ①

Now viewing Hollywood as a rival, the Fifth Generation are unwilling to acknowledge their learning from Hollywood. They would cite Chinese directors like Fei Mu, rather than Hollywood directors, as their mentors②. Occasionally, the frustration they experienced dealing with Western critics and festival committees affects their attitude toward the West in general. Once Zhang Yimou bluntly claims, Americans "don't understand foreigners' feelings"③, and "they are unable to understand the deep metaphysical frustrations of the characters [in "Raise the Red Lantern"], but I think they

---

① Lan Zuwei, "Zhang Yimou Expresses Feelings Through Overseas Phone Call," *Lianhe bao* (*United Daily*), May 26, 1994: 5.

② "Cinematographer's Exposition," in *Huashuo huangtudi*: 288.

③ Lian Taichun. "About *Red Sorghum*: Zhang Yimou Answers Audience's Questions in Nanjing," *Guangming ribao* (*Guangming Daily*) May 6, 1988: 3.

can understand the superficial ones. For me that is enough."[①] Chen Kaige also maintains, "there is a huge gap between Chinese and Westerners."[②]

In the last decade, as this kind of sentiment developed, a new term came into being: "Hollywoodism" ("Haolaiwu zhuyi"). Whenever this term is used, a disapproving overtone is added to the examinations of American films; once the entertainment is politicized, the differences of tastes become the conflicts between cultures. The term "Hollywoodism" is new but the resentment is not. The distrust between the East and the West has been mutual and historical. As Jay Leyda points out, "In the same way that Chinese worried about the portrayal of Chinese in foreign films, Europeans worried about the opportunity to see European and American selfportraits on Asian screens."[③]

Throughout human history, people from different nationalities have been prone to find faults with other cultures. To some extent, it is natural and understandable, and it is not always negative, because a thoughtful artist's finding fault in other peoples' cultures will eventually lead to the examination of his own culture. Zhang Yimou's film "To Live" is based on Gu Hua's novel. The novelist is able to relate the hardship of a black farmer in America to the suffering of Chinese people. Gu Hua says:

> I heard an American folk song "Old Black Joe." An old black slave has suffered all his life and all his family members have died before him, but, without a single word of complaint, he still views the world kindly. That song moved me deeply, so I made up my mind to write a novel. That is *To Live*, which depicts the ability of a human being

---

① Lawrence Chua, "Red Flag: China, Zhang Yimou, and *Raise the Red Lantern*," *OffHollywood Report*, Winter, 1992: 73.

② Bernice Reynaud, "Distant Mirror: The Cinema of Chen Kaige," *The Independent*, Oct 1992: 28.

③ Jay Leyda, *Dianying: An Account of Films and the Film Audience in China*: 33.

to tolerate hardship and to maintain an optimistic attitude toward the world.①

Chinese film scholars' opinions about Hollywood are historically complicated and diversified because some of them are reflective of personal views and researches and others are dutiful as official assignments. Comparatively speaking, however, Chinese artists' and scholars' views in the 1990s are less influenced by politics, but governmental views are still political. Unable to separate Hollywood from the American government, official media in China launched a campaign against Hollywood, accusing it of serving "reactionary forces". Several times, Hollywood was berated by *the People's Daily*. *Outlook*, an official Chinese magazine for overseas Chinese, censured Hollywood with extreme language.②

Contemporary Chinese critics, either conservative or liberal, tend to over-read Hollywood films. In an analysis of the ten Hollywood films that were legally imported to China③, Wang Tao thinks those films exhibit "modern people's desire to overcome the bondage inflicted upon them physically and spiritually by modern society ... In "True Lies" the heroine finally fulfills her dream of becoming a CIA agent. It is really a heroic challenge to the banality of daily life."④ Furthermore, the author politicizes Hollywood's treatment of family and marriage positively:

> "The Bridge over Madison County" is the most commendable of

---

① Preface to *To Live, Collection of Yu Hua's Works.*: 2947.

② "Hollywood Raised a Rock Only to Drop It on Its Own Foot," *Liao Wang* (*Outlook Magazine*), 1998, 7:46.

③ Ten is the maximum set by the Chinese authority for of Hollywood films to be imported to China annually.

④ Wang Tao, "Reading the Ten Imported Films from the Perspective of EastWest Culture," *Diangying yishu* (*Film Art*), 1997, 3:79.

> the ten films. It provides us with the tenderness of classical romanticism, when male and female relationships in the contemporary West are troubled by Aids. Westerners are now returning to the affections of their classical era to rescue themselves and their culture.①

The most interesting part of Wang Tao's comment lies not in his definition of Western classicism but in his speculation about the modern West. After a half century's official rejection of American family and social values, he now believes that "The Bridge of Madison Country" and the other nine Hollywood films are "concerned with contemporary issues ... in protecting the earth [ecology], the family, and the human race." In Wang's opinion, these Hollywood products are "more profound than Chinese films made by Zhang Yimou et al." and they will help "usher in a brand-new era for Chinese film and art."② Wang may sound generous in his appraisal of the ten films, but their impact in China was indeed stronger than in America. It was almost revolutionary in China, where extramarital affairs had been considered sinful, a film like "The Bridge of Madison Country" was not only forgiven but also esteemed. In spite of the government's efforts, when China opened its door for economic reasons, the influence of Western morals can no more be shut out. "The Bridge of Madison County" aroused a nationwide discussion, because it provided Chinese with a fresh moral standard that was more contemporary and more humane. In "The Epiphany of Modern Love: An Analysis of The Bridge over Madison County," Zhang Dong extends his appreciation for "The Bridge of Madison County" to other Hollywood domestic themes and summarizes them as means for a new kind of escapism:

---

① Wang Tao, "Reading the Ten Imported Films from the Perspective of EastWest Culture," *Diangying yishu* (*Film Art*), 1997, 3:79.

② Wang Tao, "Reading the Ten Imported Films from the Perspective of EastWest Culture," *Diangying yishu* (*Film Art*), 1997, 3:83.

> From "Kramer vs. Kramer," "Terms of Endearment," "Ordinary People," "Fatal Attraction" to "The Bridge of Madison County," all of them promote a single theme: to cherish love and family.... How do they cope with the boredom of day to day life? Is there a way to excite them without hurting their families? Yes, there is one: film. Film is at its best when it takes the risk on behalf of the masses. On one hand, it satisfies the audience's subconscious yearning for adventure and excitement, providing them with an outlet for their emotions; on the other, it does not present any danger to real life①.

Actually, Hollywood has done nothing new. It has always tried to satisfy the audience's yearning for adventure and excitement by fabricating dreams for them.

A century has elapsed. The quintessence of Hollywood remains unchanged, but China's response to Hollywood has changed many times. Since 1989, studies on American cinema have become more specific and no longer confined to Hollywood format. Films made by female directors, independent directors, and minorities (especially by directors of Chinese origins such as Ang Lee, John Wu, and Wayne Wang) have gained more attention from the Chinese film circle. The term "Hollywoodism" invented by Chinese film critics has been defined and redefined. An objective evaluation of Hollywood seems to be taking shape in China, because some Chinese professionals are now able to reexamine not only Hollywood but also themselves. Wang Chaoguang lists three official reasons for anti-Hollywoodism in China during the last century: First, Hollywood promotes "decadent Western cultural concept"; second, it is commercially oriented; third, it hinders the development of Chinese films, but "from a more open-minded perspective," he proceeds,

---

① Zhang Dong, "The Revelation of Modern People's Love: Analytical Appreciation of *the Bridge over Madison County*," *Dianying yishu*, 1996, 4: 86–7.

"we may reach different conclusions":

> ... in the past the so-called "pornographic" films may have included those that had shots of [girls in] swimming suites. But our standards have changed tremendously. American films may not be perfect and they do contain certain contents that are not appropriate in the Chinese context. Nevertheless, they enable Chinese people to learn about the unique aspects of Western culture. Their art and technique please Chinese audience and set examples for Chinese filmmakers. In the exchanges between China and foreign countries, they play a role. It is justifiable for American film companies to make money if the market competition is fair. . .. [In China] artists have tried hard to resist the negative influence of Hollywood and to promote Chinese films. Entrepreneurs have argued that as long as [Chinese] films are well-done, they will have an audience, no matter if we import American films or not①.

After China was admitted to WTO, Hollywood films entered China more freely—for a period of time. A time Chinese government expected cautiously, Chinese audience waited for gladly and impatiently, and Chinese film circle anticipated with mixed feelings. Chinese opinions about Hollywood will be even more diversified. No matter how this is going to happen, it, like the Chinese entrance to WTO, will be beneficial for both China and Hollywood.

In 2002 Wu Tianming, the Godfather of the Fifth Generation, directed "CEO" ("Shouxi zhixingguan," the first feature film that portrays a high-ranking American official passively). Believing that the major obstacle in the progress of the Chinese cinema was the poor quality of the screenplays

---

① "A Study of American Films on Chinese Market in the Years of the Republic of China," *Dianying yishu*, 1: 59.

and Hollywood's experience was worthy of learning, Wu Tianming organized an "Advanced Seminar of Sino-American Screenwriters" in 2008. It was conducted in Xi'an China. Teachers of that seminar included Janet Neipris from NYU Tish School and Richard Walter from Film Studies at the University of Southern California as well as such renowned Chinese screenwriters as Lu Wei and Wang Xingdong. They taught more than 100 young Chinese screenwriters for two weeks. Their lectures were collected in *Open the Door* published by Chinese Film Press. It was Wu's wish to conduct more seminars in that nature but his untimely death prevented him from doing so. Now Wu Tianming's touch is carried on by his daughter Wu Yanyan. So far, as the Supervisor of Wu Tianming Foundation, Yanyan organized five screenplay seminars to learn from important filmmakers not only in America but also in other countries.

Mulan's Transnational Identity in Disney's *Mulan* (1998) and Jingle Ma's *Hua Mulan* (2009)

HU Wei *

中文摘要 20世纪以来,(花)木兰,这一极具传奇色彩的中国女性典范形象被迪士尼影业多次改编并搬上了世界舞台,也引发了国际大众对其跨文化形象的关注和解读。本文聚焦当代中美电影中对木兰及其故事的改编,特别是迪士尼动画电影《木兰》(1998)和马楚成导演的《花木兰》(2009)。结合梳理不同时期的木兰形象、故事及其所代表的道德理念和价值取向,旨在分析不同背景和语境下,不同特质的木兰形象是如何被改编、重塑,但又相互继承发展且相互作用影响的。同时,探讨在国际视域下东西文化的传播中,"传统木兰"如何逐渐演变成为融合了自由主义热情、爱国主义精神、国家境界和世界情怀的"现代木兰"。

关键词 木兰;电影改编;跨文化形象;世界情怀

Although it was delayed by the pandemic, the live-action drama film

---

* 作者为美国南卡罗莱纳大学比较文学博士,北京语言大学外国语学部讲师。

Mulan directed by Niki Caro finally made her debut in September 2020. As an adaptation of Disney' 1998 animated film of the same name, it was Walt Disney Pictures' another practice to present the figure of Mulan based on Chinese folklore "The Ballad of Mulan" on screen.① Compared with the 1998's *Mulan*, which was beloved as the '90s Disney cannon, the latest version of Mulan has received more harsh reviews and controversial comments. Despite of the controversies, *Mulan* (2020) kindles viewers' enthusiasm for this Chinese legendary female figure once again, and further arouse interpretations of Mulan as a cultural icon.

My paper focuses on movie adaptations about Mulan in the United States and China in the twenty-first century, especially the Disney animation *Mulan* in 1998 and Chinese movie *Hua Mulan* directed by Jingle Ma in 2009. By comparing the images of Mulan and her stories in different historical period of time, I argue that as a culture icon, Mulan and her stories vary in relation to different historical and cultural contexts. While the story is retold, the image of Mulan is remolded, the morality and ethics she represents are also reshaped. But at the same time, the various presentations of Mulan interact with each other, which creates a modern Mulan marked by a feature of discontinuity within continuity. In a global society, which is characterized by the "dynamics of interaction and overlap that operate both within the global and the national and between them" (Sassen 216), and in the process of travel beyond national boundaries—from the East to the West, then comes back to the East, the Chinese legendary figure Mulan changes from traditional model of a filial daughter, a brave heroine, and a feminist to a concrete individual and a rooted "cosmopolitan patriot" (Kwame Anthony Appiah). By transcending from her Chinese identity into a transnational figure in the broad globalized community, Mulan presents a new form and expression of

① In 2005, Disney released *Mulan II*, but the story was far away from "The Ballad of Mulan".

coherence on liberalism and patriotism, nationalism and cosmopolitanism.

The Figure of Hua Mulan in Chinese Literary History

Hua Mulan or Mulan, which appeared sometime between the fourth and the sixth centuries, is a legendary figure in Chinese literary history. The earliest written account of Mulan is commonly acknowledged as an anonymous folk ballad, entitled "Mulan Shi 木兰诗" (The Ballad of Mulan) in Northern Wei period, which was first transcribed in *Gujin Yuelu*《古今乐录》(Musical Records of Old and New) edited by Shi Zhichen 释智匠 in the sixth century, and later this ballad was collected by Guo Maoqian 郭茂倩 in *Yuefu Shiji* 乐府诗集 (Music Bureau Poems, Songs and Lyrics Collection) during the eleventh and twelfth centuries. In this three hundred and thirty-two words narrative style ballad, Mulan is portrayed as a filial and courageous daughter. To protect her aged father who has been conscripted by the imperial court from the suffering of battles, she disguises herself as a male adult and joins the army to serve in her father's position. After years of fighting in the battlefield and serving in the army with merits, she turns down a promotion in the official ranks along with the benefits bestowed on her by the emperor, and would rather go back to her hometown in order to fulfill her duties of serving her family. After reuniting with her family, Mulan changes back into her feminine dress. When she presents herself in front of her male soldier friends, they are all astonished by Mulan's female identity and hasten to show their respect and applaud her for her courage and accomplishments.

Without any details about Mulan's family background, her military performance in the battlefields and her personal life, this ballad provides a large space for readers and writers to portray their own Mulan with elaboration and imagination. The sketchy portrayal of Mulan's experiences also enables varied interpretations of values and ethics implied by the character and her unconventional behavior. As a result, the story of Mulan has been retold, adapted, and represented in various literature formations, such as Chinese poetry, prose, drama, stage performances, and movies since pre-modern China.

In pre-modern Chinese culture, Mulan embodies a collection of ethical and moral values. The image of Hua Mulan as a filial daughter is regarded as a model who fully displays one of the traditional Confucian virtues—*xiao* 孝 (filial piety). She not only performs her duties and responsibilities well in supporting her family, but also concerns herself with her father's wellbeing and sacrifices herself when her father is in a dangerous situation. In addition, once she goes outside home and involves in social activities, she is able to bring honor and fame to her family. In Tang Dynasty, a prosperous and influential era of Chinese poetry and prose, several poems modeled on Mulan's story appeared, including the poem "Mulan Ge《木兰歌》" (Song of Mulan) written by Tang poet Wei Yuanfu 韦元甫 (?–771). According to Dong Lan's study, Wei's work "contributes to the development of Mulan into a model heroine by adding details that enhance the drama and underscore her virtues of filial piety and loyalty" (Dong 62).

After Tang Dynasty, Mulan and her tale not only continued to be a significant theme in poems, but also flourished in plays in Ming Dynasty and novels in Qing Dynasty. In the sixteenth century, Xu Wei 徐渭 (1521–1593), an influential poet, artist and opera writer of the Ming Dynasty, also known as Xu Wenchang 徐文长, composed a play entitled *Ci Mulan Tifu Congjun*《雌木兰替父从军》(Female Mulan Joins the Army Taking Her Father's Place), which is probably the earliest dramatization. In this two-act short play, Xu portrayed Mulan as having an elder sister, a little brother and her family name was 'Hua', and told Mulan's story in a coherent and complete manner. In the seventeenth century, the figure of Hua Mulan as a dauntless heroine appeared in Chu Renhuo 褚人获 (c.1630–c.1705)'s novel *Shuitang Yanyi*

《隋唐演义》(Romance of Sui and Tang Dynasties), in which the portrait of Hua Mulan is more elaborate with her image of a matchless brave and sagacious army leader. Fighting against the enemy without fears and hesitation, and protecting her country with enthusiasm and patriotism, Hua Mulan presents another traditional Confucian virtue—*Zhong* 忠 (loyalty).

As an iconic figure, Mulan has been regarded as not only a considerate and filial daughter to her father at home, but also a fearless and devoted soldier for her nation at the battle fields. The image of Mulan as a strong and brave heroine and patriot was further enhanced when China was under foreign invasions, especially during the period of anti-Japanese war. Because of the presentations and adaptations by many artists, such as Mei Lanfang 梅兰芳, the most famous Peking opera performer in modern Chinese history, in 1926; Hu Shan 胡珊, cousin of the famous actress Hu Die 胡蝶, in 1927; Li Dandan 李旦旦, one of the first group of female pilots, in 1928; and Chen Yunshang 陈云裳 in 1939, both the figure of Mulan and the story of were well known to almost every household in China.

After the establishment of the People's Republic of China, the new government began to encourage people to break the backward traditional conventions and practices. Mulan becomes a great example for promoting gender equality and respect for women. The image of a woman being a warrior on the battlefield or in martial confrontation breaks into the gender separation that requires women to stay inside the female living quarter. What's more, Mulan further displays her courage and claims her female agency while she marches into a conventionally masculine territory where she equals or sometimes outwits and outperforms her male contemporaries. In 1951, Chang Xiangyu 常香玉 presented the story of Mulan in Yu opera, in which she emphasized the important roles women played in the society. In the story, when General Liu criticizes that women do not contribute to the protection of the country, Mulan responds with objections:

> What Brother Liu has said does not make sense. How come women enjoy idle lives all the time? While men are serving in the army and fighting in the front, women are working at home villages without any rest. They farm in the field in the daytime and weave at home during the night. It is because they work diligently around the clock that the soldiers can have food to eat and clothes to wear. If you do not believe it, please look at ourselves. From the shoes and socks to the coats and trousers, all are hand made by women with one needle after another. In the history, there are also many heroines who bravely fight for the country and provide meritorious services. Who can say that women are inferior to men? (my translation)

The theme of "women can hold half of the sky" further highlighted in the movie *The Red Detachment of Women*（红色娘子军）directed by Xie Jie（谢晋）in 1962. While these women soldiers get together and march to the front, they sing their anthem loud and proud,

> March on, March on!
> The soldiers take great responsibilities,
> The women suffer from deep rooted unfairness.
> In the past, Hua Mulan joined the army in her father's place,
> Nowadays, the detachment of women will carry guns to protect the people. (my translation)

The late twentieth century witnessed the dramatic changes in Chinese society since China carried out the Open-up and Reform policies. The flourish of movies and television industry also provided more stages and channels, such as television series, to present Mulan and her stories with more illustrations and creations. In addition, with the enhancement of international communication, more and more people outside China are able to know the figure of Mulan and imagine her stories. As a matter of fact, Mulan's story has already traveled to the West since the late nineteenth century, but it is the success of Disney's animation enlists Mulan in the Disney Princess family and introduces Mulan into the global market.

Mulan's Introduction in the United States

The legend of Mulan has enlightened all kinds of literary products in China, but its cultural influence does not limit to the East. In terms of the image of Mulan, a similar trajectory of her as a filial daughter, a heroine to a feminist can also be found in the process of its introduction in the United States from late nineteenth century to the twentieth century.

In 1894, W. A. P. Martin published a book entitled *Chinese Legend and other Poems*, which was possibly for the first time that Mulan was introduced to the English-speaking West. Under the title of "Mulan, the Maiden Chief," Martin translated the story based on "The Ballad of Mulan." In the 1930s, Chinese American poet, playwright, and novelist H. T. Tsiang combined Mulan's legend with a true story and wrote a three-act play with the name of *China Marches On* and staged in New York City and Los Angeles during 1939 to 1944, with the purpose of arousing the sympathy and supports from the working-class American audiences to their fellow workers who were struggling against Japanese imperialism in China. Tsiang's woman warrior—Mu-lan Chung—is separated from her parents during the Japanese invasion of Shandong in 1914 when she was an infant. When she grows up as an adult, she leads a suicide squad to resist the Japanese invasion of Shanghai in 1937.①

---

① A brief study on H. T. Tsiang's *China Marches On* can be found in Floyd Cheung's article "H. T. Tsiang: Literary Innovator and Activist." *Asian American Literature: Discourses and Pedagogies* 2 (2011) 57–76.

Although Mulan's story circulated in the United States in the first half of the twentieth century, it was Maxine Hong Kingston's publication *The Woman Warrior: Memoirs of a Girlhood among Ghosts* in 1976 that made the story of Mulan into wide acknowledgement. Using a first-person narrative, Kingston retells Mulan's story, which not only breaks Mulan's historical boundary and represents Mulan's story with her own Chinese American experiences, but also complicates this legend with more issues such as female subjectivity and sensibility.

Disney's Mulan: Seeking for the True Self and Personal Happiness

In 1998, fascinated by this Chinese version of Joan of Arc, Disney produced an animated film *Mulan*, which brought the figure of Mulan into the visions of global audiences with new interpretation. In this animation, Mulan is presented as an unique girl who is eager to find her true self and longing for happiness and fulfillment in her own way.

Disney's Mulan reflects the conventional understanding of an eastern beauty—a slim girl with phoenix eyes, arched eyebrows and a cherry-shaped mouth. To emphasize Mulan's Chinese identity, Disney also deliberately concentrates many Chinese elements into this animation. The animation starts with a close-up gaze of the distinguished Chinese landmark—the Great Wall. Chinese musical instruments are used for the theme songs to highlight Chinese lyrics; traditional Chinese brush drawings and paintings as well as Chinese architectures are introduced into background decorations and settings. Mulan's mansion is characterized with a typical Chinese style gate, roof structures and backyard garden, which are all portrayed in colors as the Forbidden City, a piece of Qing Dynasty style architecture. Even though Mulan is anachro-nistic—she dresses up in Sui Dynasty style clothes, with Tang Dynasty's decoration, her Chinese image is vivid and conspicuous.① These delicate and elaborated designs break Disney's conventional technical routines with fresh eastern atmosphere. What's more, it has been stereotyped that animals are indispensible in Disney's animations, so in *Mulan*, a dragon or a lizard-like dragon and a cricket accompany Mulan during her adventures.

Together with these symbolic elements, certain Chinese family cultural values and traditions are stressed in the animation as well. Mulan grows up in a big harmonious family with her parents and her grandmother. In the most beautiful place at the courtyard of Hua mansion, is an ancestral temple, where they can easily worship their ancestors and pray for blessings and protection. These distinguished oriental features and Chinese values are surely attractive to global audiences, especially Western audiences. But along with these highly valued merits in eastern culture, Disney's Mulan story also enhances some widely recognized desires in western traditions, such as to pursue personal freedom, happiness and success.

At the beginning of this animation, Mulan's family sets her up on a blind date with great expectations. However, she fails to gain the matchmaker's favor and is driven out of the meeting place. Mulan's behavior not only disappoints her parents, but also is marked as a disgrace of her family's honor, because girls are expected to bring honor to her family through marriage. The Matchmaker scolds at Mulan: "You may look like a bride, but you will never bring your family honor!" Deeply ashamed at her failure to "uphold her family's honor" in the only way traditional Chinese society deems possible, Mulan sighs: "Look at me. I will never pass for a perfect bride or a perfect daughter. Can it be that I am not meant to play this part? Now I see.

---

① In the article entitled "A Cross-cultural perspective on Production and Reception of Disney's Mulan through Its Chinese Subtitles," Jun Tang discusses the reorganization of the Chinese elements in this animation in details, especially in terms of the inappropriate cultural traditions, historical unsuitability and linguistic non-Chinese elements. *European Journal of English Studies* Vol. 12, No. 2, August 2008, pp. 149—162. ISSN 1382–5577 print/ ISSN 1744–4243 online.

If I were truly to be myself, I would break my family's heart." Facing her reflection in the pond, using the gravestone as a mirror, Mulan wipes off her cosmetics on the face and struggles with her eagerness of finding her true self. She asks:

> Who is that girl I see staring straight back at me?
> Why is my reflection someone I don't know?
> Somehow I cannot hide who I am, though I've tried.
> When will my reflection show who I am inside? ①

To utilizing a mirror as a device of revealing a true "self" actually can be traced back to "The Ballad of Mulan." In this ballad, after Mulan comes back to her home from the battlefields, she changes her battle suits back to her female clothes in her own room, and she says:

> "I open the door to my east chamber,
> I sit on my couch in the west room,
> I take off my wartime gown
> And put on my old-time clothes."
> [Then] Facing the window she fixes her cloudlike hair,
> Hanging up a mirror she dabs on yellow flower powder. (Frankel 70)

Whereas the traditional Chinese Mulan recovers her true self—the female identity—in the mirror with the "yellow flower power," which reveals her femininity, Disney's Mulan is eager to search for her true self—her individuality instead of femininity—in the mirror with the gesture of getting

① The quotations from Disney's *Mulan* are all cited from the scripts of this animation. For the complete script, see http://www. fpx. de/fp/Disney/Scripts/Mulan. html.

rid of the cosmetic mask on her face. This adaption and contrast further emphasizes the pursue of Disney's Mulan, that is to seek for a true self and to defend family honor through her talents instead of her marriage. Believing that "the flower that blooms in adversity is the most rare and beautiful of all," Mulan decides to disguise herself as a boy under the name of Hua Ping and to take her father's position in the army. She regards this action as an opportunity to protect her father and to fight for her family's glory. More importantly, she perceives it as a way to pursue freedom and happiness. It turns out that as Disney's Mulan fully displays her talents, abilities and wisdom in her military life, she also earns her love of her free will. Contrary to the Mulan in the ballad, who manages to hide her female identity from her fellow soldiers until the end of the war, Disney's Mulan accidentally reveals her female identity after she gets injured in a battle. Instead of driving her away from the army, General Li Xiang acknowledges Mulan's courage and wisdom, and does everything in his power to protect her. Their mutual admiration and fondness gradually grows into love. After they defeat the enemy and return to the capital, the Emperor personally approves their marriage.

Disney Mulan's behavior can be better understood in American culture, because "American culture is... held to be individualist, [and] litigious... obsessed" (Appiah 627). For many Americans that "American core—and, in particular, the attachment to the constitutional order and the rights it conveys—is not what centers their lives.... What they desire centrally, what shapes their lives, is what the American freedoms make possible" (Appiah 628). The Chinese society where Mulan historically existed, on the contrary, was dominated by paternalism and Confucianism. For thousands of years, men were the masters of the world and dominated the society with power and authority, whereas women were confined to home, marginalized and subordinate without any control over their own lives. The traditional Confucian values promote the ideology of "three obediences" (to father before marriage, to husband after marriage and to sons after the death of husband) and "four virtues" (morality, proper speech, modest manner and diligent work) as the standards on how women should behave. This orthodoxy provides men with great powers and firm superiority within the family and the society. As a result, women could not, and never would, be granted the right to pursue freedom, let alone to seek free love without obstruction.

Rooted in Chinese cultures, Disney's Mulan has to follow the social moral requirements and fulfill her duties to her father and her nation, but at the same time, she revives another "self", a self that Disney adds to Mulan's traditional Chinese identity, a self that breaks the cultural boundaries by granting herself the ability and power to break orthodox restrictions and search for her own well-being. By interpreting Mulan's action of joining the army as a brave move to fight for her family as well as for herself, Disney poignantly inserts a new concept into the figure of Mulan who "has been historically constructed as overwhelmingly national" (Sassen 218). It also establishes a powerful bond between Chinese culture and Western philosophies, between the cares for others and the considerations on individual interests, between dutiful responsibilities and independent minds, as well as between conventions and passions. Consequently, the figure of Mulan enters into the global sphere with her transnational identities and unique characteristics.

Jingle Ma's Hua Mulan: Caring All People as a Cosmopolitan Patriot

While Disney enjoys the $300 million revenue① brought by *Mulan* and claims its huge success in molding the character Mulan as "one of the most

① See http://www. oocities. org/hollywood/5082/boxoffice. html.

recognizable symbols of Chinese culture"①, Chinese producer Guo Shu, executive president of Starlight International Media Group, responds with "a sense of national responsibility" and announced that "[n]ow that foreigners can produce a popular movie out of the story Hua Mulan, why can't we Chinese present its own to the world?" ② Funded by mainland China and directed by Hong Kong director Jingle Ma, the Chinese live-action movie *Hua Mulan* premiered on November 2009 in mainland China, Singapore and Malaysia with a future plan to negotiate for release in United States and Europe.

Influenced by Disney's interpretation of Mulan as a daring girl who desires for personal freedom and happiness, in this Chinese movie, the understanding of Mulan also breaks the boundary of traditional presentations which limit Mulan merely as a filial daughter and a dauntless soldier. Jingle Ma's portrait of Mulan emphasizes on her feminist sensitivity—love and care, towards her father, her soldiers-in arm, and her nation—as well as the fear of war and the extended concerns of all the innocent people involved into the war.

Since Qing Dynasty, most heroes or heroines in Chinese literature are tend to be portrayed as sober and serious people instead of sentimental or romantic ordinary persons. Jingle Ma's Mulan, however, is a sentimental person, and this personality has been reinforced throughout the movie. As the only child who lost her mother when she was young, Jingle Ma's Mulan lives with her father and keep each other company. Mulan takes good care of her father, but also worries about his health. Whenever she sees her aged father staggering with his legs, which have been wounded in the battlefields, or hears her father's heavy coughing, she cannot help sighing sadly with knitted

---

① Ling Woo Liu, "China vs. Disney: The Battle for Mulan", Hong Kong Thursday, Dec. 03, 2009, http://content. time. com/time/world/article/0,8599,1944598,00.html#ixzz2etRm655l.

② Ling Woo Liu, "China vs. Disney: The Battle for Mulan", Hong Kong Thursday, Dec. 03, 2009, http://content. time. com/time/world/article/0,8599,1944598,00.html#ixzz2etRm655l.

brows. She also cares about the people in her village, especially her neighbor Fei Xiaohu whom Mulan treats as her younger brother ever since childhood. After Mulan joined the army, she also shows kindness to her comrade-in-arms by consoling the soldiers who miss their sick parents and sharing their worries. Despite the fact that the ruthless war consumes people's physical energy and destroys people's mental vitality, Mulan and her soldier friends try to take care of each other and spiritually support each other to survive the brutal battles. Among these friends, General Wen Tai is the only man other than Fei Xiaohu, who also joins the army and helps her cover her female identity among the male soldiers, knows her true identity. Unfortunately, their friendship grows into a kind of ambiguous romance with a tragic ending.

Jingle Ma's Mulan, like Disney's Mulan, also accidentally exposes her female identity to General Wen while she bathes naked at night in a hot-spring unaware that General Wen is also bathing there. In the darkness, General Wen discovers her sex but not her identity until a later incident when Mulan takes the blame for the theft of a wallet in order to avoid a body search. These incidents provide opportunities for Mulan and General Wen to further get to know each other and gradually fall in love. However, unlike Disney's Mulan, who eventually lives a happy life with General Li ever after, Jingle Ma' Mulan and General Wen have to conceal their true feelings even though they both know how much they love each other. They have to sacrifices their happiness because General Wen has to marry Rou Ran Princess in exchange for the peace for all peoples between the two enemy countries. Although Jingle Ma's Mulan does not gain a happy marriage, Mulan's sentimental entanglement with General Wen makes her a vivid human being with passions and love instead of an emotionless heroine in traditional portrayal. The presentation of Mulan as a pubertal girl longing for love is further stressed at the end of the movie. Before General Wen marries Rou Ran Princess, he visits Mulan at her hometown. Mulan finally opens her heart to him with tears: "You are the only person that I will never ever forget. In the past twelve years, to think of you is the first thing that I do when I wake up in the morning. Because of you, I have the courage to open my eyes and start every day. Even though we will never be able to see each other again, I will never stop thinking of you from now on."

Jingle Ma's portrayal of Mulan as a sentimental human being also lies in to reveal her fears and concerns instead of illustrating her as an invincible and merciless solider. During the first engagement with the enemies, Mulan cannot bear to kill the solider until the general gave her the military order. The moment she cuts off the head of the enemy soldier, Mulan is stupefied by the bloody scene. She questions the action of killing and fighting while washing off the blood on each soldier's dog tag. Regardless of the warnings from General Wen who claims that "there is no place for emotions on the battlefield" because "the feelings will make people become too soft-hearted to fight against each other", Mulan struggles against thus warrior mentality. Having experienced too many cruel battles which took the lives of her comrades and friends, Mulan refuses to continue combat. "I do not want to fight.... In my heart, I am a person afraid of war".① Despite of her fears, Mulan joins the army out of her desire to protect her father, and once she becomes a soldier, she shoulders her obligations to protect her nation and would die to protect her homeland without hesitations.

Jingle Ma's Mulan is surely a patriot, but her loyalty to one nation, does not rule out her beliefs on moral justice to all of humanity. In the battlefields, Mulan extends her concerns to people who are beyond her kin or compatriots. In a sense, she is a cosmopolitan patriot. On the one hand, she loves her homeland; on the other hand, her "loyalty to humankind—so vast, so abstract, [so] a unity—does not deprive [her] of the capacity to care for lives nearer by" (Appiah, "Cosmopolitan Patriots" 622). It is her fears of war

① The quotations from Jingle Ma's *Hua Mulan* are all my translations.

and her concerns of people from all nations that make Mulan would rather sacrifice her own happiness to achieve a better world for all people. As she claims, "if I can use my life in exchange for the peace among all the people, I will surely do it."

Like Disney's Mulan, Jingle Ma's Mulan is a sensitive and sentimental individual who longs for love and happiness. But Jingle Ma's Mulan also extends her love and concerns to the people in general. Her belief of sacrificing oneself for the greater good further highlights the vital merits in Chinese culture and conveys the call for peace beyond one nation.

Disney's Mulan and Jingle Ma's Mulan: Promoting a Peaceful World within the Nation and beyond

One important reason that Mulan, both Disney's Mulan and Jingle Ma's Mulan, joins the army is to protect her nation from the invasion of enemy army. The word "nation" stems from the Latin verb *nasci*, "to be born". It originally designated a group of people who were born in the same area (Zernatto 351–366). It was not until the 16th century, with the wake of democratization process in England, that the term "nation" became synonymous with "people" for the first time. Gradually, this term transformed into a modern national concept with multiple aspects, including relationships with cultures, economies, social and political structures (Dieckhoff and Jaffrelot "Introduction"). Conservative nationalism places an emphasis on the collective dimension of human life, and regards collectivity, the ethnic group or the nation, is the sole unit for nationalism analysis. In spite of the varieties existing within the nation, nationalists still believe that it is a consolidated and united community which they belong to. Cosmopolitanism, to the contrast, is based on individualism, and it puts the morally autonomous individual at the center of its philosophical consideration. But it does not mean that a person cannot be a nationalist and cosmopolitan at the same time, because while one attaches with his/her nation, he/she can also extend the moral emotions to the larger scope—the world at large.

As a mixture of Chinese elements, Disney's animation simplifies the enemy to Mulan's nation as Xiong Nu Army. But the happy ending of this story is not just about defeating them in the battlefields. It is also related to how people can enjoy a happy and peaceful life. In the animation, Mulan wittily defeated the enemy army led by Shan-Yu twice. The second combat happens at the capital when people are gathering together to celebrate the victory. However, the joyful atmosphere is interrupted by the sudden invasion conducted by Shan-Yu and his three soldiers, who soon take control of the imperial hall. To save the Emperor and the people in the city, Mulan, changed back to her woman dress, enters the imperial hall together with three close male soldier friends who disguised as maids-in-waiting, and eventually subdues Shan-Yu by her intelligence. The Emperor is saved and the people resume their happiness in singing and dancing.

In contrast to the hilariously happy life enjoyed by Mulan and her fellows in Disney's animation, the peaceful life promoted in Jingle Ma's movie requires more efforts and struggles, because the concept of "nation" is more complicated due to China's historical situations. China is a country with a great amount of ethnic groups. From the late fourth century to the middle of the sixth century, China was a place comprised of different nations because it was divided into several states dominated by different ethnic groups. Along with the Tuo Ba branch in Xian Bei（鲜卑）ethnic group which established Northern Wei State, Mulan's home nation, there were at least four other main ethnic groups—Xiong Nu, Jie, Di, and Qiang—co-existed. The Rou Ran people, whose army Mulan and her troops fight against in Jingle Ma's movie, are one branch of Avars ethnic group. The name Rou Ran in the Altay language means "foreigner," and indeed they are foreign to Northern Wei people. In Jingle Ma's movie, this "foreignness" is implicitly emphasized by the fact that Vitas, the famous Russian singer with the nickname of "Prince of Dolphin Voice," serves as an important servant to Rou Ran Khan①. Contradicting to people of Northern Wei State, which occupied the central area where people live a stable life on farming and handcraft operations, Rou Ran people live a nomadic life in the grassland without settled cities or villages. Lack of the knowledge of farming and productive skills such as making ironware, they have to move around depending on the seasons and rely on animal husbandry and hunting. Besides different life styles, Rou Ran people and Northern Wei people are also different in religions and political structures. Whereas most of Northern Wei people believe in Buddhism, Rou Ran people promote Saman religion. Ruled by a Khan, Rou Ran is a military state full of aggressive equestrian nomad warriors. Due to the shortage of stable living resources and the ambition for the territory domination, Rou Ran Khan often leads his army to invade the Northern Wei State over wealth and power.

As a matter of fact, when the purpose of a war is about the scramble for power and control, it is usually the people who suffer most in the war. Consequently, the desire of establishing a peaceful world is beneficial for people as a whole, which is stressed in Jingle Ma's movie by portraying Mulan as an anti-war individual and a peace defender. In the movie, the ferocious Rou Ran Khan Mao Dun challenges Mulan and insults the Northern Wei army by saying that "We, Rou Ran people are wolves, unlike you Northern Wei people are only sheep." Mulan calmly replies: "There are Han people, people from Qiang ethnic group, Di ethnic group, Xian Bei ethnic group and Xiong Nu ethic group in our army; but no sheep!" In contrast to Mao Dun, who distinguishes people from different ethnic groups or nations with

① The director Jingle Ma says it "was a simple marketing decision", but the result is that the "foreignness" is even obvious and reliable.

racial discrimination into different hierarchies, Mulan treats people from different ethnic groups as human beings and extends hospitality with regard to "the right to the earth's surface that belongs in common to the totality of men" (Kant 118). In Louise Edwards' words, Jingle Ma's Mulan "becomes a defender of peace and a reluctant warrior since she abhors killing and the needless violence war inflicts upon innocents and soldiers alike" (Edwards 212). Mulan fully acknowledges the differences between people of her nation and that of Rou Ran ethnic group. Not only were they different in habits and customs, but also in languages, cultures and ideologies. In spite of this, she still treats them, especially the soldiers, as people who are forced to drift into wars due to the leaders' avarice of power and wealth, and believes that all people should have the right to live a peaceful life.

In Jingle Ma's movie, Mulan's yearn for a peaceful world also ignites her to seek for harmony with practical actions. When General Wen is captured by Rou Ran Khan as a hostage, Mulan dresses like a Rou Ran woman and persuades Rou Ran Princess who also would like to stop the inhuman and cruel war to assist her in killing the tyrannical and aggressive Rou Ran Khan Mao Dun. With the death of Mao Dun, not only is General Wen saved from the Rou Ran prison, a chance to stop the wars between the two nations also emerges. Having suffered from the poverty and chaos caused by the wars for so many years, people from both Northern Wei and Rou Ran look forward to better and peaceful lives. When it turns out that General Wen is actually the Prince of Northern Wei State, instead of eloping with General Wen, Mulan encourages him to marry Rou Ran Princess as a way of bonding the two nations and making peace for all the people. In *Perpetual Peace*, Kant suggests that a valid treaty of peace should not reserve issues for a future war (Kant 341). In pursuing "perpetual peace," even if it may be not perpetual, Mulan and Rou Ran Princess both agree on a simple peace treaty—political marriage—between the two nations. Such a peaceful development is not confined to the simple recognition on the coexistence of multiple identities, but extends to the interaction between the national and the global identities transforming in a positive way. As Sassen points out, "[t]oday social actors are likely to live, and entities likely to operate, in overlapping domains of the national and the global" (Sassen 221). Mulan accepts the differences among nations with openness. She also believes that once the foreigners connect with a certain kind of bondage, self and other are united. By exchanging each other's resources and cultures, such as exchanging commodity and surviving skills, a kind of "context hospitality" can be enjoyed by people both from Northern Wei State and Rou Ran cross boundaries, instead of being treated as an enemy upon arrival in another's territory (Kant 118).

Poshek Fu views Jingle Ma's movie *Hua Mulan* as "a strong projection of" China's desire of being "part of the global community" with concerns "over soft power right." In certain degree, Jingle Ma's Mulan subtly projects the "peaceful development" foreign policy promoted by the Chinese government since 2003. On December 3, 2003, during the Boao Forum for Asia, Zheng Bijian, the former Vice Principal of the Central Party School, first proposed the term of "peaceful rise." In his speech, Zheng put forward three crucial strategic principles: (1) "unswervingly advance economic and political reforms centering on the promotion of a socialist market economy and socialist democracy;" (2) "boldly draw on the fruits of all human civilization while fostering the Chinese civilization," and (3) "carefully balance the interests of different sectors, securing a coordinated development between urban and rural areas, between different regions, between society and the economy, and between man and nature" (Zheng 18). Zheng believed that in today's new world, China should "strive for a peaceful rise," and work "toward a peaceful international environment for the sake of our own development and at the same time safeguard world peace through this process of development" (Zheng 18). To avoid the possible perceptions that China is a threat to the established order brought by the word "rise", at the

2004 session of the Boao Forum, Chinese president Hu Jintao changed the phrase to China's "peaceful development." As China gradually emerges as a great economic, political and military power, China wants to ensure other countries that its development will not be a threat to peace and security. By internally harmonizing China' society and externally promoting a peaceful international environment, China seeks to avoid unnecessary international confrontation and would like to cooperate with other countries in establishing a world order for the benefits of people on earth.

Despite that Jingle Ma's movie echoes these principles, I, however, argue that this movie also reflects a concern on how to present nationalism in the cosmopolitan world. In the age of globalization, despite the tendencies of homogenization, westernization, or cosmopolitanism, the concept of nation-state does not shrink away, but is enriched with simultaneously accelerated negotiation and interpretation on cosmopolitanism and nationalism. Kok-Chor Tan argues that "cosmopolitanism, as a normative idea, takes the individual to be the ultimate unit of moral concern and to be entitled to equal consideration regardless of nationality and citizenship" (Tan 1). He further claims that "the incompatibility between liberal nationalism and cosmopolitanism disappears once we get clear the parameters of liberal nationalism and the scope of cosmopolitan global distributive justice" (Tan 107). Paul Jay also perceives, "(o)n the one hand, migration, the media, and global capitalism are appropriated and adapted from a shared westernized pool of images, fashions, foods, and music, and on the other hand, older historical forces related to longstanding territorial, ethnic, and religious disputes continue to fuel nationalist aspirations and identities, resulting in a dizzying production of new states and nations" (Jay 118). Jingle Ma's Mulan interprets this coherence of liberal nationalism and cosmopolitan through her simple understanding and practice of "justice without borders" (Kok-Chor Tan) with cosmopolitan consideration. She regards the world she lives in as a big family with people from different branches, therefore the equality should be applied to all people as a whole, and the harmony should also be achieved through the cooperation and understandings among all the people.

No matter in Disney's animation or in Jingle Ma's movie, Mulan's sentimentality, her longing for a better life, and her actions of promoting a harmonious world all contribute to the image of Mulan as a peace defender.

Joseph Chan claims that "Mulan has become a transcultural text: a combination of old and new, traditional and modern, East and West, collectivism and individualism, female submissiveness and women's liberation" (Chan and McIntyre 241). Since the twentieth century, this Chinese legendary figure comes into the world stage via Disney's animation with a transnational identity. Her sentimental understanding of selfness and otherness places her into a position transcending her from a bounded nation to a large global community. While in its travel from the West back to the East, she further appears as a cosmopolitan and peace advocator with Chinese characteristics in Jingle Ma's movie. Rooted in Chinese culture, Mulan displays the filial piety to her father, the loyalty to her home country, but at the same time, she transcends her nationality and citizenship with the care for people beyond her own compatriots and the belief that the peaceful life belongs to the whole human community. As a significant cultural icon, Mulan, as well as her stories, surely will continue to travel in the global world with more interpretations.

Works Cited

Appiah, Kwame Anthony. "Cosmopolitan Patriots." *Critical Inquiry* 23.3 (1997): 617–639. *JSTOR*. Web. 13 Oct. 2013.

Chan, Joseph Man. "Disneyfying and Globalizing the Chinese Legend Mulan: A Study of Transculturaion." In *Search of Boundaries: Communication, Nation-States, and Cultural Identities*, edited by Joseph Man Chan and Bryce Telfer McIntyre, 225–48. Westport, Conn.: Ablex, 2002. Print.

Cheung, Floyd. "H. T. Tsiang: A Critical Overview of His Work in Literary and Social Context." *Asian American Literature: Discourses & Pedagogies* 2.0 (2011): 57–76. *onlinejournals. sjsu. edu*. Web. 26 Apr. 2014.

Dieckhoff, Alain, and Christophe Jaffrelot. *Revisiting Nationalism: Theories and Processes*. London: Hurst, 2005. Print.

Dong, Lan. *Mulan's Legend and Legacy in China and the United States*. Philadelphia, Pa: Temple University Press, 2011. Print.

Edwards, Louise. "Transformations of The Woman Warrior Hua Mulan: From Defender of The Family To Servant of The State." *NAN NÜ* 12.2 (2010): 175–214. *booksandjournals. brillonline. com*. Web. 26 Apr. 2014.

Frankel, Hans H. *Flowering Plum and the Palace Lady: Interpretations of Chinese Poetry*. New Haven: Yale Univ Pr, 1978. Print.

Liu, Ling Woo. "China vs. Disney: The Battle for Mulan", Hong Kong Thursday, Dec. 03, 2009. Web.

Jay, Paul. *Global Matters: The Transnational Turn in Literary Studies*. Cornell University Press, 2010. Print.

Kant, Immanuel. *Perpetual Peace, and Other Essays on Politics, History, and Morals*. Hackett Publishing, 1983. Print.

Sassen, S. "Spatialities and Temporalities of the Global: Elements for a Theorization." *Public Culture* 12.1 (2000): 215–232. *CrossRef*. Web. 25 Apr. 2014.

Tan, Kok-Chor. *Justice without Borders: Cosmopolitanism, Nationalism, and Patriotism*. New York: Cambridge University Press, 2004. Print.

Tang, Jun. "A Cross-Cultural Perspective on Production and Reception of Disney'S Mulan through Its Chinese Subtitles." *European Journal of English Studies* 12.2 (2008): 149–162. *JSTOR*. Web. 26 Apr. 2014.

Zernatto, Guido. "Nation: The History of a Word." *The Review of Politics* 6.03 (1944): 351–366. *Cambridge Journals Online*. Web.

Zheng, Bijian. *China's Peaceful Rise: Speeches of Zheng Bijian, 1997–2005*. Washington, D. CC: Brookings Institution Press, 2005. Print.

Online Recourses

Disney's *Mulan* scripts. http://www. fpx. de/fp/Disney/Scripts/Mulan. html.

Ling Woo Liu. "China vs. Disney: The Battle for Mulan." Hong Kong Thursday, Dec. 03, 2009.

http://content. time. com/time/world/article/0,8599,1944598,00.html#ixzz2etRm655l.

The Exploration of Self in Wu Tianming's Films

LUO Dan *

中文摘要：如何对待中国的传统和现代性是吴天明电影的重要主题之一。很多学者在研究中突出了吴天明是如何将二者冲突化处理的。本文从“自我观”这个角度出发，探讨吴天明电影中所呈现的“我”。这个“自我”既包括角色主体，也包括体呈“自我”的符号，如土地、脸谱和唢呐。首先，吴天明无意将传统和现代完全对立，乃至于倡导一种非此即彼的选择态度。《人生》中的“内省我”，《百鸟朝凤》中的“体知我”，以及《变脸》中的“童心我”都在不同层面表达了吴的“自我观”。其次，吴天明表明“现代我”的失败在于对启蒙式“自我”的一种理想化实践。他在此基础上指出一个多样但不冲突的“现代我”的前提，即如何克服主客分裂的世界观。这源于吴对“真我”的考量，其作品实际是对“真我”的情境化演绎。正因为主体的自主性源于关系结构中的“真我”，传统和现代的对立在这里就迎刃而解。

关键词：吴天明；自我；传统与现代；真我

* 作者为美国南卡罗莱纳大学比较文学专业在读博士，主要研究领域为中国电影。

Introduction

One of the central concerns in Wu Tianming's films is the conflictual tension between the sweeping force of China's modernization and the inheritance of traditional values. Many studies address this tension by analyzing these two sides in his particular films. Therefore, previous research has meticulously explained how Wu criticizes the alienation effects of China's modernity in the 80's context, and on how he laments the bygone existence of traditional community and its cultural representation.① They argue that Wu characterizes the effacement of traditional ethics as the consequence of China's modernization project.

Thus, Wu's films are understood as presenting modernization as the ultimate villain, ruthlessly invading a self-contained entity and eroding its ancient beliefs. Even though scholars do recognize Wu's "Godfather" role in the history of Chinese cinema, they do so by shaping him into a single-handed fighter for the beauty and revival of rurality. Hence, there has been too much analysis on why the admirable efforts of saving the tradition are accomplished successfully in some films (*Life* and *King of Masks*) and poorly in some others (*Song of the Phoenix*).

This paper does something different. First, I treat the conflictual tension between modernization and tradition in Wu's films not as a question of causality but as a symptom of the evolving modern subjectivity. Second,

---

① Many essays written on Wu Tianming's films are based on the understanding that Wu has a clear-cut representation of Chinese tradition and modernity. Some examples that are relevant to the films in my discussion include Guo 2016, Meng 2019, Qin and Yang 2017, Tang 2016, Yang and Liu 2017, etc. While these essays are particularly illuminating in how Wu depicts the precarious status of tradition and how he shows the negative aspects of modernity, they seldom approach his films in terms of how the protagonists perceive themselves in this transitional moment of Chinese society. This is why my essay focuses on Wu's conception of the self in times of great change.

I show how Wu's films can be read from the perspective of an evolving modern subjectivity, instead of an either/or-choice over types of sociality. In particular, I treat the multiple characters as different aspects of Wu's conception of the self. Consequently, the cultural symbols—such as the land in *Life* (1984), the technique of face-changing in *King of Masks* (1996), and the instrument Suona in *Song of the Phoenix* (2016)—are representatives of this self. In a way, they *are* the characters of the films and embody the change of self because they constitute the sign of the modern subject's existential crisis in such times.

I argue that the seemingly irreconcilable conflict between the tradition and the modern is Wu's way of dramatizing the characters' life-changing choices in order to highlight the painful transformations of the modern self. Instead of condemning that which is foreign, Wu, in fact, endeavors to provide answers to the following questions: why do personal adaptations to a new set of social norms succeed and fail? What options does the self have in a transitional time? How can tradition empower the transformation of self? This paper shows his explorations and answers in three films: *Life*, *King of Masks*, and *Song of the Phoenix*.

Tested in *Life*: The Failure of the Introspective Self

Wu's film follows the story of Lu Yao's novella *Life* (1982). The main character Gao Jialin is a village-born intellectual, whose choices in career and love relation ended tragically. Song Fengying explains that his tragedy is a result from both Gao's personality and the insurmountable boundaries between the countryside and the city in the early 1980s, during which time China had just started its politico-economic reform (2013). Gao Jialin represents the conflict between rural and urban because his life is determined by the rural/urban side he lives, not by his capability as an intellectual. Thus, his choices made on one side may have irreversible consequences.[①] Song continues to argue that the prices he pays become especially heavy when it was his high self-esteem and even selfishness that determined these choices (e. g. accepting nepotism to get the job in the city), rather than ethics and principles.

But the kind of ethics and principles we speak about here—devotion and loyalty to the community—seem to confine Gao to his rural identity every time when he is about to become an urbanite. That is, these ethics serve to limit his upward mobility. I content that Gao's actions come from his questioning of such ethics and principles, although he does so painfully, struggling with his own conscience.

My analysis then turns to how his inner self is represented through these struggling moments of introspection. This section argues that Wu Tianming's *Life* in fact accentuates the conflict between two kinds of self. One kind of self is found in Qiaozhen 巧珍, whose identity is embedded in rurality and nourished by the soil and the labor. Wu's camera, by showing her innocence and almost unconditional love, celebrates her beauty that is the very product of the soil. Thus, she forms a sharp contrast to Gao Jialin 高加林, who represents the other kind—what we may call the introspective self.

The film begins with Gao's return to be a peasant because he has just lost his teaching job at the village school to the son of the Party's secretary. The son Sanxing 三星 has no desire to learn or teach. In the past, he had to rely on the favors delivered by his high-ranked father to even get a basic education. Here, Gao is introduced as an ambitious youth who feels disconnected to the rural life and wishes to change his fate through knowledge. He wants to be treated as an intellectual, different from those who are neither talented

---

① Lu Yao makes this point clear: "One's life is indeed long, but there are only a few crucial moments, especially when one is young." (人生的道路虽然漫长，但紧要处常常只有几步，特别是当人年轻的时候。) Quoted in Song.

nor have any desires for knowledge. When he moves to the city to become a journalist, the audience follows this journey moving back and forth between two identities—the rural peasant and the urban dweller. Wu Tianming invites the audience to contemplate on the differences between the two through Gao's voice-over, the inner speech that exposes the critical moments of Gao's self-evaluation. For example, when he stops by the city after having lost his teaching job, we hear his thinking out loud: "I must come here. I am as educated and cultured as the other young people in this city. Why do I have to endure this humiliation?"

In this scene, we watch Gao evaluating his knowledge and capability, affirming the possibility of change, and then deciding to abandon the rural roots that equal humiliation. The humiliation he speaks of means precisely the seemingly unchangeable identity as a peasant worker. The first day when he goes back to labor after the lay-off, he states that "I want to taste all the bitterness so I would not fear anything in the future." The rural land is a place of bitterness that devours personal endeavors. What makes life meaningful here is the collective devotion to the land, whereas moving to the city and becoming a journalist is not only empowering but also transforming: "I am no longer the son of the peasant. I am no longer a passerby." These moments, again, are told in Gao's voice-over.

Such moments show that Gao's self is intimately associated with introspection—that is, the power of his action is found within himself; for him, it is the individual that creates the meaning of life. A better life results not from the decision made by people around him, but from the handcraft of the individual.[①] Gao Jialin's determination of abandoning the rural mentality is contrasted with the older generation, his parents, who merely accept the

① As Descartes famously pointed out in *Discourse on Method*, nothing counts as knowledge unless the subject has successfully doubted it. In this line of thought, one is only a subject insomuch as he takes thinking upon his own being.

reality of his replacement because of the prevalence of nepotism around them. The fact that Wu opens with this scene is telling—he is pointing out that introspection, a quality that characterizes modern subject's existence in Western Enlightenment thought, can be readily found in 80s' rural China, albeit in only a few. Gao is one of those who believe in the incompatibility between rural collective life and personal growth. The cornerstone of such belief, however, comes from the introspective self, a concept deeply embedded in China's early twentieth-century political thoughts and intellectual history. It is beyond the scope of the current study to trace how the concept of self has changed along the lines of Enlightenment agenda and anti-traditionalism. Suffice it to say, however, that the modern sense of self, precisely defined to discredit the self one finds inside of rural Confucian community or traditional family, continues to "lure" individuals to break free of such confinements. In the 80s' context where the market reformation gradually started to revive the cities, to break free means to break down the severe rural-urban stratification.

Thus, Wu's version of *Life* is an experiment on how liberating this "enlightened" self is when the negative and backward aspects of rural culture remain a constraint of individual freedom. The introspective self fails to cross the rural-urban boundary because he cannot conceptualize a subjectivity beyond this binary. His existence is an either/or question. We can see that Wu presents this self as something irreconcilable with the rural environment. To make it possible, Gao has to adopt the interests of the urban and abandon both his rural roots and Qiaozhen's love. This makes his return to the village in the end very bleak, as he is shown walking alone in the winter, knowing Qiaozhen has married someone else. The man who abandons becomes the one who is abandoned by both the urban and the rural identity. The failure of the autonomous self, then, does not lie in its lack of strength to pursue a good life, but lies in the symbolic discrepancy in between the two spaces.

Between the Collective and the Social

Traditional concept of inter-subjective relation has long been critically studied by intellectuals ever since the Late Qing period. In May-fourth literary representations, familial values such as filial piety and obedience are revealed as cannibalism.① Individualism is supported, worshiped, and implemented. This, along with the appearance of a consumer society in the '20s and '30s, gives rises to bourgeoisie liberalism. Although both individualism and liberalism would become the target of criticism in the CCP-led decades, they do not simply disappear upon the arrival of Maoist ideology. On the contrary, the collective mind seems to embrace these values more than before since after the 1980s, especially with the rapid development of a market economy that signals a retreat of state control in everyday life.

The consequences are twofold. On one hand, urban areas are developed at the cost of the rural population's welfare. This is achieved by a top-down regulation of agriculture and industry. The result is that the division between the urban and the rural becomes wider and deeper. There is a collective idealization on both sides: urban life is elevated, envied, and privileged; rurality is idealized in nostalgic discourses that shape it as the idyllic other. On the other hand, because of the need of developing private ownership, stories of individual heroism and the mechanism of competition remain prevalent. They reinforce such beliefs and the illusion that one can achieve mobility by crossing over the thin line of rural and urban.

Obviously, there is a conflict. Should one believe that pursuing individu-

---

① These examples are easily found in literary representations from the May Fourth period and New Culture movement. One either walks out of the family (Ba Jin) or becomes the madman in the village (Lu Xun).

al interests can overcome the class stratification along the rural/urban binary? How does one navigate between the told illusion of individual heroism and the nation's agenda of sacrificing rural development for the benefit of the urban? This conflict is especially salient for Gao Jialin, who wholeheartedly believes that education can make him the master of his identity. But born in a poor village in Northern China, he is a peasant for life. It is within this context that every choice of his becomes crucial. In other words, Gao Jialin is caught in between his conversion to the collective belief and the social reception of such belief.

Liu Xinmin's differentiation of the collective and the social is helpful here. When talking about the possibility of self-realization outside the "liberating" values of the Western individualism, he argues the following:

> Whereas collectivity avails itself of the disposal of ideologically and organizationally hegemonic powers such as the CCP-led modern state, sociality refers to a deeper, vaster and thus murkier nexus of relationships shaping the social sphere of the family, the public and other groupings. (36)

Sociality thus comprises much wider collective beliefs and ideologies that transcend historical epochs. Caught in between, Gao's individualism becomes something instrumental, selfish and uncivil. This is why Wu Tianming's film presentation became highly controversial upon its release. To the audience, it is unacceptable that he prioritizes self-interests, especially when Qiaozhen, the representative of the pure and innocent rurality, has to be sacrificed in his pursuit of an urban life. I would argue here, however, that Gao's betrayal appears unethical to many audiences because his choices challenge the traditional understanding of interpersonal relations, which remains centripetal to rural sociality at that time.

This idea is presented in Qiaozhen's character, whose self is built in relation to the land and the pride she takes in labor. Her femininity is atypical in terms of her capability, daring, and vision. In her imagined future with Gao, she is the one who provides for the family: "I won't let you 'eat bitterness'…you can stay home." Later she adds, "I will let you have Sundays just like the school days." But her femininity is also typical in the sense of sacrificial womanhood: "Why don't you go out (to the city) to work? I will stay at home to farm and raise our kids." How do we reconcile these two seemingly contradictory sides?

First, we have to forego the "intuition" of understanding femininity as a lack of masculinity. This, again, derives from a modern representation of self through sexuality. Second, Qiaozhen should be understood in contrast to the land, not to the man. In Wu's mise-en-scène, the poetics of the country life is found in her movements across the fields and the folk songs she sings. Her beauty is most powerful when placed against the background of the vast, openness of the rural landscape. The land is part of Qiaozhen, and Qiaozhen a part of the land. Though she is not educated, she is cultured. She is, in every way, the cultural product of the soil.

Wu thus negates the femininity/masculinity binary. Behind Qiaozhen stands the rural self Wu imagines: one knows her identity through communal relations to others and to the biotic world. By putting herself into the other's space and determining what is needed from her, Qiaozhen does not know a dualistic perception of I/Other. Wu proposes a self that can be more open, fluid, and free, and all of these have nothing to do with conforming to the life of an urbanite. This is what makes Qiaozhen a memorable figure in Chinese cinema. Her character upholds autonomy, an assertive self that is in harmony with her rural sociality but by no means selfish—the traits that the audience may easily pin to the urban characters such as Hunag Yaping（黄亚萍）, Gao's latter girlfriend, and Kenan's（克南）mother, who called him out for his own love interest in Yaping. We might even relate this self to the classic Confucian understanding of *shu*（恕）. Translated as reciprocity (Du Weiming), forbearance (Lin Wusun), or even altruism (Feng Youlan), *Shu* entails what it means to be a unique individual in one's multivalent relationships.①

The audience's responses, judging from the controversies surrounding the film at that time, testify to the discrepancy between the collectively advocated individualism and a sociality that still believes in traditional ethics. Gao is unfortunately the victim of such discrepancy, especially at a time when his rural origin was considered the inerasable "core" under the Household Registration system (Hukou 户口).② When the audience thought along with the confinement of the system, Gao was blamed for his betrayal to Qiaozhen—that is, the rural self he was supposed to embrace—or, find a way to negotiate through, rather than casting it aside.

Of course, there is no moral judgement from Wu Tianming himself. The film remains sympathetic to Gao's character throughout. But it does not have a naïve take in giving a possibility to the union of the two identities—instead, Qiaozhen marries to another peasant while Gao's future in the village is left uncertain.③ This take reveals a tendency of Wu's abandonment of the introspective self, which, as argued above, reflects an Enlightenment

---

① Feng Youlan defines *zhong* (*chung*) 忠 and *shu* 恕 as two aspect of the Confucian core value *ren* (*jen*) 仁 . "'Do to others what you wish yourself.' This is the positive aspect of the practice, which was called by Confucius *chung* or 'conscientiousness to others.' And the negative aspect, which was called by Confucius *shu* or 'altruism,' is: 'Do not do to others what you do not wish yourself.' The practice as a whole is called the principle of *chung* and *shu*, which the way to practice *jen*" (Feng 43).

② Established in the 1950s, the Hukou system classifies every registered person as either "rural" or "urban." The classification is closely associated with state welfare and other social benefits one could receive.

③ In Lu Yao's novel *Life* (1982), when Gao Jialin goes back to the village and feels humiliated as well as disheartened, the villagers emerge from the corn field and embrace his return with kindness and warmth. Wu did not include this detail in his ending. Gao is seen walking alone to the black soil in winter with his back to the audience. This take may have already suggested a dualistic interpretation between the urban/modern kind of self and the rural one. We will see this tendency most clearly in *Song of the Phoenix*, where the traditional music and the erosion of Western orchestra are depicted as rivaling and even hostile.

understanding of the individual's relation to other and the society. In his disappointment, Qiaozhen's image is idealized to represent the forgotten value of traditional intersubjective relations. This following section continues to trace Wu's representation of such self in *Song of the Phoenix*, now in the image of Suona. Wu insists on looking for empowerment from the community at a time in which both the collectivity and the sociality would seem to have chosen Gao's type of self-perception.

The Collapse of Rites and the Spoilt of Music

Upon the release of *Song of the Phoenix* two decades after *Life*, an individualist ideal hardly poses any dilemma to most of the young people in the film *Phoenix*. The pursuit of a better material life at the cost of the rupture of collective tradition seems fairly reasonable among the young. It is only a monstrous crime in the eyes of Jiao San（焦三）, who is perhaps the last Suona（唢呐）master in a northern village. In this section, I first answer the question why the authority of Suona and the music diminish at the turning of hands. I then locate the deeper issue of the rural community's disintegration in Wu's view. Because he thinks that Suona is the symptom of the disintegration of communal values, I argue that such treatment signals his refusal of the vulgarized "reconstruction" of tradition in China's culture industry after the 1980s.

We could ask Wu Tianming, why a film about Suona? Suona is an important means of living to some northern communities, like the one in the film. But for Wu, it is also a metonymy for things that used to unite or integrate a community, things now from which we now witness its bygone power. The film discusses this process by telling a story of inheritance. The young You Tianming（游天鸣）is introduced in such light, as someone who is trained since his childhood to become a potential new master. Hence, watching him undergo specific training, we learn the importance of embedding oneself in the art history and life-long experiences of the instrument. In fact, the film contends that it is the history of Suona itself that has created the cultural identity and authority, as well as its transcendent existence tested throughout time.

Jiao San is venerated as the master of this music because the history of the traditional Suona practice endows him with this authority. The film stresses that Jiao San underwent almost brutal training and grew to be the only Suona master who can continue to teach disciples. The camera zooms in on the heavy box that stores Suona of different sizes, while Jiao explains the history of authority behind them. The audience learns, with Tianming, the personal stories of ownership: "this piece was made in the Qing dynasty and has a history of several hundred years; that piece is what I inherited from the grandmaster of my master…" We are to understand that Jiao lives to hold up the history of rituals and to eventually pass them on. In a funeral scene, Jiao insists on finishing the piece at the sacrifice of life—his blood drips out of the instrument, confronting us with the painful efforts in sustaining this tradition. Jiao San *is*, in fact, the instrument Suona and the classic songs. The master is thus to be understood as the extrinsic authority of the instrument at a particular time. In sacrificing his life for the practice, Jiao turns his death into the spiritual symbol of Suona.

But it is more than spiritual. Jiao is also the master of ethics in the eyes of the local. The Suona profession is seen as a practice of rites from which the craftsman's self-cultivation is achieved. Using his own knowledge, the master thus has absolute authority in judging the moral achievement of the deceased. The film presents the funerals and weddings in northern rural China as the most important socializing occasions. When Jiao performs with his crew, they are always highly respected—not just for Jiao's master identity but more importantly, because the collective values represented by

Suona should be venerated. When the village people host funerals, it is up to the Suona master's decision whether to perform *Song of the Phoenix* or not. This is the final judgement that functions as an education to the local. The performance of the classic Suona songs at such emphasizes and consolidates the crystallized values regarding what is morally good at a collective level. Here, the film locates the indispensable nature of Suona in its aesthetical and moral nourishment. Because the moral nourishment maintains healthy interpersonal relationships, Suona's continuation remains crucial to the survival of the community. Wu Tianming shares this point of view with scholars who interpret traditional art forms through their ritual functions:

> Ritualized roles and institutions, as a corpus of meaning-invested practices, preserve and transmit cultural significance. For this reason, the performance and embodiment of the ritual tradition both socializes and makes one a member of a community (Hall and Ames 32).

Consequently, when Jiao exclaims "rules broken! rules broken!", he was by no means resentful for his own loss of authority but the rupture of tradition. One is reminded of "Rites collapse and music spoilt" (*libeng yuehuai* 礼崩乐坏) in the Spring and Autumn period (771–476 BC), where the disintegration of the political and economic system was accompanied by social disorganization. When people in the village follow the fashion of inviting Western orchestra in its vulgar form, it is made clear that Suona is depleted of its stage because of these fashions. However, it is not that Suona music no longer has value; it may have a different life in the market economy. Wu is arguing that the collapse of the rural way of life and value system is the root of the art's extinction. Suona is a telling symptom.

The gradual disappearance of the crew members also testifies to the gravity of the collapse. The musicians have to support their families in other ways, and some of them choose to work on construction sites in the city.

One musician ends up losing a finger in an accident; another seems to have developed chronicle pulmonary disease for working at a tile factory. None of them can play Suona anymore. Wu treats this consequence symbolically—conscripted by the construction of a new economy, they are deprived of the ability of even picking up the instrument.

Where should Suona go? Will it have an "afterlife?" Wu probes into these questions in another very important scene, where Tianming dialogues with Lanyu 蓝玉, another Suona learner who "lost" to Tianming in the competition of becoming the heir. Lanyu talks about starting a construction team to build temples and old-style architectures. He urges Tianming to join him; Tianming, however, did not respond. Perhaps it seems ironic to him, and to Wu himself, that these musicians are working on reconstructing the "old-styles" when the inherent values supporting them are now invalid. What exactly are they building but a space depleted of any cultural reading? It is not that tradition does not have a place in market economy. Its survival, however, depends on everyone accepting its copycat form and a value limited to tourist interests. But can such forms continue traditional values and hold together a community?" Wu shows how the new economy, in the attempt to renew traditions, hollows them out.

Lament from/for the *Phoenix*: a Self to Be Reborn

Wu has a point. This is the situation shared by many other indigenous art forms in contemporary China. What is lost is not just the peculiar tradition but part of the cultural identity in that tradition, which, if handled critically, could even empower the kind of self that is lost in the modernization project. We have seen how this self can turn out to be anxious, indifferent, and even uncivil in *Life* through the urban characters. This section connects the failure of introspective self to the exploration of an embodied self. I argue that Wu sees the survival of Suona in the rediscovery of cultural values. That is, the way to keep tradition alive is to reconsider what kind of ethics it should entail and support in current situations. However, while Wu suggests the many empowering ethics from Confucius thoughts, he did not integrate this into character development, precisely because he rejects the commercial format of cultural products.①

First, the film directs our attention to a new land ethics that requires us to extend the meaning of community to the natural world. This is shown in the children's learning of Suona, which is accomplished through bodily and aesthetical experiences in nature. The disciples do not simply disengage and observe how the crew performs; the most important part of the training is rather to immerse them in the perceptual world and have them experience *nature's* sensitivity and emotion. The master is shown passing on his aesthetic experience and value in nature, and the two children, Tianming and Lan Yu also have to develop a relationship with the water, reeds and birds by themselves. They have to listen to the sounds made by nature in all seasons and learn to imitate the birds with the instrument.

In other words, to integrate Suona into oneself, one has to listen, observe and reflect on nature. This pedagogy seems to suggest the idea of embodied knowing, a thought in New Confucianism, brought forth initially by Du Weiming(杜维明). Embodied means to inherit the tradition by "accommodate [ing] and integrat[ing] everything in the world, and letting all these things become something that is non-objectified in our mind" (Hung 207). Part of the cultural values of Suona practice is found in these moments. If we contrast this with the failure of the introspective self in *Life*, the kind of self entailed in Suona practice is one integrated with the community in the broad sense of nature and human world. To Wu, this maybe the hope that enables

---

① See An Da. "The Last Twenty Years of Wu Tianming: No Trashy Films!" (安达:《找不到钱，也不拍烂片！吴天明的最后二十年》,《电影世界》, 2016(06):13–15+12.

us to overcome the dualism of I/the World.

However, the importance of embodied knowing in Suona gradually fades away as the film focuses more on the conflict between the practice of this tradition and the import of Western orchestra and pop music. These conflicts could be more shocking and Tiaming's identity more dimensional if, the thread of Suona's inner values continues to give a complete and clear set of its ideals, principles and methods for implementation. And perhaps the most important question is: how can the conduct of these standards facilitate modern subject's pursuit of a civilized and nurtured way of living? That is, how do "the values that are embodied in tradition have a significance that goes beyond their own era" (Chen 326)?

In the film, the *Song of the Phoenix* is upheld to the ultimate classic, but even so, what it stands for should not be the sole standard for assessing the values. Ultimately, the strength of development of tradition should come from both of the following sources: a complete and clear set of values found within the art form, and a strong and innovative self we can find in Tianming, whose genuine appreciation of the music ("to the bone") is highly-praised by the Master. At some point, these two sources should become one.

Similarly, there *could* have been more character development for You Tianming, who now has no other choice but to hold up the evolution of tradition in times of unprecedented challenges. The old Confucius saying about cultural continuity goes: "Maintain the old alive whilst yet knowing the new".① This is what Tianming's character could demonstrate by not just "speaking according to" the classics but more actively "speaking in continuation with" it (Chen Lai's words). To solve the existential crisis of the traditional art, it has become necessary for the heir to develop it toward a direction that provides not only moral knowledge but a spiritual path. This may contribute to break down the binary of traditional/modern, indigenous/

① *Analects* 2.11. Translation by Chen Lai.

Western. Master Jiao becomes a spiritual symbol of Suona by giving himself to the music, but Suona does not have a self unless this spirt is carried on in constant renewal, just like the reborn of a phoenix. This certainly does not mean Tianming has also to die for the cause. Rather, the path—as is shown in the last scene when he walks into the future—suggest an open-ended realm waiting to be fulfilled with new meanings, practices, and authorities. Just like how Master Jiao was venerated, the social respect for the character Tianming has to come from the action of continuing history itself.

Unmasking an Authentic Self in Changes

If there is a solution suggested to the renewal of the tradition in *Phoenix*, perhaps it is the moment when Master Jiao confesses to Tianming: "do you know why I decided to pass on Suona to you? It is because the tear you shed when your father tripped." A tear drop gives away the veneration of benevolence and familial attachment valued very much in a traditional community, but more importantly, Wu points out the origin of actions—authentic caring.

I argue in this section for a pattern in Wu's films. That is, he intends to pin down the role of this authenticity in the formation of the self. There are many examples. In *Rivers without Buoys* (1982), the river is the source of authenticity to the protagonist Pan Laowu（盘老五）, its force signifying that justice will eventually "flood" away the corruption of the land. Another example is *Old Well* (1986), where the survival of the collective is only made possible by the willing sacrifices of individuals across history. These sacrifices come from an authentic care for the villagers' life and should not be understood simply as the oppressive nature of impoverished and backward rural culture.

Masks is yet another mature exploration that signifies Wu's theorizing of a contextualized authenticity, especially at times when individuals are challenged of their sense of self. In the context of *Life*, the humane authenticity is the will to struggle; in *Phoenix*, it is responsibility; in *Rivers*, justice; in *Old Well*, sacrifice; in *Masks*, a child's mind (tongxin 童心).We may call his contextualization as *positioned* authenticity. This position is where one's authenticity locates, and from which one's acts initiate.

While this pattern of locating the position in Wu's works remains unexplored by critics, the concept of authentic feelings is hardly my invention. The cult of *qing* (情), for example, leaves us with rich resources to argue for the importance of human's sentiments and feelings as self-liberation against normative principles, such as those from Orthodox Confucianism. It is in attempting to locate this positioned authenticity that Wu looks for the dialectic relations between the self and the collective. For him, the depth and sublimity of the self is realized through one's relation with the community, but it does not mean that the individual cannot act otherwise but conform. Authentic feelings are what enable individuals to question and even change communal expectations and disciplines.

Masks is where he articulates best this dialectic relation, precisely because the example of a child's growth enables him to explore this positioned authenticity. The 8-year old girl Doggie (狗娃) is the most powerless figure of all, whom we could describe as already being abandoned by life. Yet, she has a way to "force" the more powerful to interact with her. In this process, the older generation is transformed—along with it the "normative" part of the tradition—and mutual care and love preserved. It is in this sense, in stressing on the role of authenticity in self-empowering, that the touching story goes beyond a simple melodrama, which, as Gary Susman criticized, "has the stale ring of fortune-cookie aphorisms." He continues to argue that Wu deploys a "creaky plotting" and the emotional power of the film comes from Wu's exploitation of Zhou Renying (周任莹) , the child actor who plays Doggie, "whom Wu disturbingly puts through some perilous stunts and whose character responds to all manner of abuse with heartbreaking emotional directness" (116).

I must say that critics who understand Wu this way fail to understand the film at all. And to some extent, they fail to understand what it means for other modernities to "return" to their traditions. It is not about assuming the position of Western modernity and judge China's tradition from their sense of morality, which entails the right of man, equality of all, the protection of law, etc. Instead, Wu wants to ask: where do stories of equality and rights come from? If not protected by law, how are the powerless protected in anyway? Now it is the time to learn how Doggie grows a self in constant negotiation with her surrounding brutality.

To be sure, born a girl, Doggie's miserable experience has taught her to actively fight for her survival, but it is not satisfying to attribute this to a clear understanding of self. She did not "plan" to disguise as a boy so that Old Wang will buy her; a careful audience should notice that it is an action coerced by the child-trafficker. She cares for Wang not because he is the "master," but because she loves him as "grandpa." She thus treats Wang with a child's truthfulness. The seemingly "deception" is brought forth to suggest her powerless position—as a child, she has no immediate moral judgement on how great the consequences of her actions are, in which she is forced. She learns only what is given to her. This point cannot be clearer where she imitates the self-sacrificial scene from the opera play Miaoshan-myth to plea for Wang's life. This scene has just appeared on stage to entertain the General. In his analysis of the play, Kevin Dodd argues that this myth is about the reconciliation between women's pursuit of freedom outside the traditional family and the Confucian social value of filial piety. He reads *King of Masks* in line with the morale of filial piety and interprets the relation between Doggie and Wang as still upholding the complex of filial piety.

I would argue that this dangerous act is less an internalization of the filial piety in the play than a convenient utilizing of the opera plot. In other words, even though Guowa exerts a kind of agency by herself from the beginning, she still is a convincing character in that her way of knowing and acting is in accordance with her age. She feels "real" not only because she loves the way a child loves her family, but also because it is this love that produces (fatal) mistakes.

At first, it seems that her mistakes come from ignorance. She knows how much Wang treasures the masks, yet she secretly plays with them under candle light and burns the boat, which is the means for them to live and survive. She also delivers the boy Tianci（天赐）just because she understands "Grandpa likes teapots with snouts"（爷爷喜欢带茶壶嘴嘴的）, unaware that this would lead to his imprisonment. But again, we have to think about her position—she can only act on what she learns. She thus acquires a sense of self by *causing* a relation to the objects and others around her. This is not ignorance, but unprincipled knowing. That is, she acts in accordance with her emotional responses, and not with outside rules or principles that determine how things should work. Her knowledge is thus unsystematic, unsorted and unmediated. Actions based on such knowledge are spontaneous and can be sometimes disastrous. But this is also why when she imitates the Miaoshan play and hangs herself down from the roof in exchange for Wang's life, she "performs" without the filial piety complex that is at the heart of the play. Rather, what marks this act really is her authentic caring that is not demanded by a generational code called filial piety.

It may be useful to recourse to an understanding of the child's mind. Li Zhi（李贽，1527–1602), one of the most adamant rejecters of blind belief and discipline of orthodox Confucianism, wrote specifically on the genuineness of the child's mind. In *On the Child's Heart-Mind* (*Tongxin Shuo* 童心说), he states: "A child is the beginning of a person; the child-like heart-mind is the beginning of the mind." What about this heart-mind that worth our nurturing? Li continues: "The child-like heart-mind is free of all falsehood and entirely genuine; it is the original mind at the very beginning of the first thought" (Pauline Lee's translation).① Throughout the entire film, Wu emphasizes this "first thought" as the basis of Doggie's decisions. This is why the "genuine" emotions are the source of both endangering actions and rescuing missions.

Wu thus locates in the child an emotional authenticity that transcends the ethical and familial codes in tradition. Doggie shows that the tradition can be renewed of its form by asking for acknowledgement as human being. This enables her to articulate questions such as "why am I less than a boy?" "Kuan-yin has bosoms too; why do you worship her?" The interrogation of self thus comes from Doggie's positioned authenticity, which, in the end, not only changes the inheritance rules of the face-changing tradition but also transforms the adult self who adheres to this principle.

My last point is about the representation of self through the masks. This face-change technique requires a special training of the actor's dexterity, because the actor has to change pre-painted masks in split seconds. Assuming new faces in a fast speed, then, suggests the wonder that it takes no visible transition—which we may interpret as the growth of self—to become these new identities. Such quick change of faces can also lead one to question the very language in which we talk about the self: is there an essential self behind the masks? Which one of those should be the person? Is s/he all of them, or is the identity entailed in the rapid changes? It is safe to say that assuming many masks does not mean that the self is "empty," or that "there cannot be an authentic self." In Wu's representation, face-changing becomes a symbol of the malleable self to be shaped by many forces and circumstances. It seems ironic that Old Wang, the *King* of Masks, passes on the techniques of change without realizing that change itself is necessary for the technique to stay alive.

---

① Original Chinese: 童子者，人之初也；童心者，心之初也。……夫童心者，绝假纯真，最初一念之本心也。

Conclusion

This search for the positioned authenticity symbolizes Wu's efforts to build a more humanistic environment for China's project of further modernization from the '80s on. For him, cinema should have been an effective platform to share this responsibility. Hence, it is understandable that the lament of ever-diminishing humanism in contemporary China in his films carries an undertone of education. But the cinema-goers in the new millennium, tired of political messages and accustomed to fast-fade kitsch, tend to reject the calling for critical thinking as a sugarcoat of didactic discourses. Thus, they welcome the masculine superpower in a film like *American Captain* precisely because the source of power is a given and *can* be taken for granted. Compared to its popularity, *Phoenix* falls into a presupposed suspicion of didactics. Even though the box-office of *Phoenix* suddenly sky-rocketed, it was largely because one of the producers, Fang Li, keened down for better exposure. The mass reaction the film received is a phenomenon that shows how it is the entertainment that sells, not the content itself.

I conclude with a remark of how Wu Tianming's films have participated in the cultural conservatism ever since the 1980s. First of all, cultural conservatism（文化守成主义）does not mean an conservative attitude that manifests in overtly rejection of the core ideas of modernity, such as human rights, democracy, freedom, equality, etc., and in overtly affirmation of anything traditional and of nationalist identity politics. On the contrary, cultural conservatism acknowledges the need for ongoing social reforms, whilst concerns itself with the negative consequences of rapid change and total rejection of traditional values. These consequences include the destruction of ethical order, disintegration of morally-bind community, and utilitarianized individuals. Or to put it more precisely in Chen Lai's words: the point of view of the so-called cultural conservatives with regard to culture is that of anti-anti-traditionalism and anti-pan-utilitarianism.

Second, addressing the ongoing development of marketization, industrialization, and utilitarianism, Wu uses his films to show how such rapid and unrestrained reforms result in detrimental effects on human morality and community. He participates in the cultural debates ever since the '80s, the core of which remain the "tradition-modernity" relation. The three films above attempt to answer the questions that are at the center of these debates. That is, what should be rejected from both the Chinese and Western traditions and what should be critically inherited from both.

Third, Wu Tianming's cinema contributes to the conversation of cultural debates by presenting two types of self from both sides. In *Life* and *Phoenix*, the collapse of moral order accompanies, on one hand, the disintegration of rural collectivity, and on the other hand, the flourishing of individualism and civil urbanization. The self we see here is someone who *thinks*, and calculates for benefits, but without a solid supporting moral system. But this is precisely because the kind of reason, in which they believe, strips away the traditional ethical order.

The self he presents from the side of "tradition," returns to the basic belief in human authenticity. And he argues for the many origins of this authenticity by contextualizing it in his films. Therefore, he locates the idealist traditional self in the figure of a child, who has not yet been socialized into any rigidly defined ethical orders, and can thus stand up against the sexist bigotry and blind elevation of authority in Confucian tradition and against the kind of benefit-driven self in *Life*. Wu rejects an understanding of false authenticity—being true to your feelings does not mean you are free to choice anything without consequences. An isolated and atomistic self is not an autonomous self.

The character Tianming in *Phoenix* provides a transition for us to evaluate both. At the same time, Tianming stands for Wu's own firm belief in the humanistic self, which raises nothing but the fundamental philosophical question: "What is a good life?"

Works Cited

Chen Lai. *Tradition and Modernity: A Humanist View*. Brill, 2009.

Confucius. *Analects*. Edt. by R. Dawson. Oxford University Press, 2008.

Dodd, Kevin. "*King of Masks*: The Myth of Miao-shan and the Empower of Women." *Journal of Religion and Film*, vol. 16, iss.1, 2012, pp. 1–23.

Feng Youlan. *A Short History of Chinese Philosophy: A Systematic Account of Chinese Thought from Its Origins to the Present Day*. Edt. Derk Bodde. The Free Press, 1948.

Giles, James. "The No-Self Theory: Hume, Buddhism, and Personal Identity." *Philosophy East and West*, vol. 43, no. 2, 1993, pp. 175–200.

Hall, David and Amers, Roger T. *Self, Truth, And Transcendence in Chinese and Western Culture*. State University of New York, 1998.

Hung, Andrew Tsz Wan. "Tu Wei-ming and Charles Tylor on Embodied Moral Reasoning." *Philosophy, Culture, and Traditions*, vol. 9, 2013, pp. 199–217.

Lee, Pauline. *Li Zhi, Confucianism, and the Virtue of Desire*. State University of New York Press, 2012.

Liu Xinmin. "In the Face of Developmental Ruins: Place Attachment and Its Ethical Claims." In *Chinese Eco-Cinema*. Edt by Mi Jiayan and Sheldon H. Lu. Hong Kong University Press. pp. 217–233.

Susman, Gary. "The King of Masks." *The Village Voice*, vol. 44, no. 17, May 1999, p. 116.

Yang Guorong. *The Mutual Cultivation of Self and Things: A Contemporary Chinese Philosophy of the Meaning of Being*. Indiana University Press, 2016.

Wu Tianming and Chinese Cinema: The Field of Cultural Production since 1979

HU Tingting *

中文摘要 本文从“文化生产”角度入手，理解吴天明作为艺术家和电影厂管理者的双重身份，并以此来解析当时制作一部好电影的意义。本文认为吴天明在其所处时代中国电影文化生产场域里承担了关键角色，作为文化能动者，他的重要性由两方面体现：第一，作为一个电影制作者，吴对于新型审美的艺术创造在《老井》登顶，这一关键特征丰富了中国西部片电影制作人在“寻根”氛围下持续的影像想象；第二，作为西安电影制片厂的管理者，吴天明充分支持了艺术家的自主权，对有潜力的导演提供经济支持。如此，吴天明的艺术创建和行政措施为当时的文化场域参与者提供了三种资本：艺术资本、经济资本和政治资本。

关键词 吴天明；中国电影；文化生产；中国西部片

This paper first deals with the theoretical issues embedded in cultural production theory in Chinese studies and then outlines the basic paradox

* 作者为美国南卡罗莱纳大学比较文学专业在读博士，主要研究领域为中国电影。

and features of post-Cultural Revolution Chinese cultural production, accompanied with an in-depth analysis of how Wu's role of head of Xi'an Film Studio as the cultural agent confronts the historical, economical, and political predicaments that in return allows filmmakers, including himself, autonomy. Then, this paper looks into the blossoming scene of the Chinese Western and considers how Wu's role as a filmmaker has contributed to the historical task of inventing new visual imaginaries for this new genre, with an exemplary case study of *Old Well*. This paper ends with a brief look at Wu's film trajectory, commenting on the differences of filmmaking before and after the coming of capitalism.

The Theoretical Predicament

To understand the complex cultural production scene in modern China, Michel Hoakx has applied French theorist Pierre Bourdieu's theory of cultural production to the reading of modern Chinese literature, inspiring more insights into the interactions and complexity of the production of culture. However, there are also other concerns about this theoretical approach. Scholars such as Wendy Larson and Haiyan Lee have pointed out the problem of displacement and the doubt on a structuralist analyzing method. Larson questions "the validity of applying Bourdieu's notion of 'habitus' and 'field' and cultural and symbolic capital to Third World nations that are only beginning to develop capitalist-style economies" (qtd. in Mabel Lee 161). Haiyan Lee contends that whether "the economic logic of maximizing material and symbolic profit exhaust the range of actions and goals that agents pursue in the cultural field" (qtd. in Michel 2012; 49). In response, Michel Hoakx contests that "the complexity of human agency" and of the field are never denied by Bourdieu, rather Bourdieu holds that these are significant matters but that "the objective existence of long-standing structures and relatively stable positions ensure that much human agency is in fact predictable and can very well be reduced to a smaller number of principles" (51).

Nevertheless, Hoakx maintains that Bourdieu's models of cultural analysis and has edited a book contributed to reading Chinese modern literature in light of Bourdieu's theoretical approach. With this, Hoakx argues that "Bourdieu's ideas have also inspired critical reflection on the past, present and future of the Chinese socialist literary system, raising questions about the relationship between the literary field and the field of power" (56). It is important to note here that the fact that Bourdieu's theory continues to inspire works of discussion on Chinese cultural analysis and offers vocabulary for us to approach cultural products are in themselves proof of the everlasting and present value of engaging in a Bourdieusian analysis of more cultural products. Historically, the introduction of Bourdieu's theory started in 1979, from an article that touched upon the subject (55). Continuously, more and more scholars engage with the conversation and "Bourdieu's model of the literary field and the interaction of capital, habitus and position is employed most enthusiastically in 'contextual' studies aiming to present a broader overview of literary production of any given period, or to rehabilitate previously ignored or marginalized authors, works and trend" (56). By focusing on the cultural agents' "autonomy" from "two heteronomous principles, namely 'politics' and 'the market,'" Hoakx concludes that the successful production of an idea relies on workings among "symbolic capital, economic, and political capital" (52). By including the cultural production scene with a focus of films in post-Mao era, I wish to join the ongoing conversation of Bourdieu's analysis and lay out the new possibilities it prompts for us to deconstruct the workings of the complex factors at scene of filmmaking in Post-Mao times. Studying the case of Wu Tianming, I highlight the interaction of the cultural agent with the economic and political capital, considering the space for relative autonomy and the possibility of collective agency.

This part, drawing on Michel Hoakx's development of Bourdieu's theory, views Wu Tianming as a cultural agent whose film career has reflected the discursive scene of contemporary Chinese cinema under the post-Mao cultural production system. As Michel "suggest[s] that successful trajectories inside the modern Chinese literary field involve a careful balancing act between striving for critical recognition (symbolic capital), for political efficacy without sacrificing independence (political capital) and for discreet money-making (economic capital)," this paper will read Wu through historical records of his career as a director and as the head of Xi'an Film Studio and analyze his films and the relation he has with the production of Chinese cinema (52). Special attention is paid to the relative autonomy of the cultural agent as both a director and a sponsor, which revolves around three capitals. The methodology I use is what Bourdieu describes as "thick description," which, in the cultural studies sense, would be a close reading of the multiple layers that have together weaved the net for a successful production of a film. Therefore, a careful consideration into the historical background, political context, the role of each cultural agent and their interaction with each other, the display of each element in the ultimate visual image, and the ideological predicament will all be part of the scrutinization.

This paper believes that a reconsideration of Wu's critical role at the scene of post-socialist cultural production demonstrates a rewarding message to the understanding of contemporary Chinese cultural production, which is even more caught up between an interaction with state censor (political capital), market (economic capital) and symbolic capital. Ultimately, this paper argues that the blossom of a period of wonderful cultural production, exemplified by the new genre (Chinese Western), largely relies on the relative autonomy provided by Wu's role as the power-holder, who has interacted with economic, and political capital but resisted and exerted his own power, for a nationalist pursuit of better art. His interaction with the two capitals, which stems from his firm belief in art, has formed a positive habitus of the

5th generation filmmaking and the field. The success in symbolic capital on a global stage also in return acts in the form of collective agency that further benefited the field.

Wu's Administration at the 1980s Cultural Production Scene

Politics has been vital to Chinese modern cultural production and one primary purpose of cultural products. From the eyes of the political cultural products are to serve its ideological advocations. At the very beginning, the Chinese socialist literary system was established in "communist-controlled areas of China during the War of Resistance against Japan (1937–45) and the Civil War that followed it (1945–9)," and later it was made nationwide after "the founding of the People's Republic in October 1949" (Hockx 56). This system at first largely imitated the Soviet system where "literary production was planned and controlled by national and regional propaganda departments and by party committees inside publishing houses, as well as by an overarching state organization known as the All-China Federation of Literary and Artistic Circles, one of whose subsidiaries was the Writers' Association" (56). This system also influenced the cultural production even after the extremes of the Cultural Revolution. Evidently, in the design of the system, "the primary relationship, which all the other relationships were supposed to support, was that between top leadership and readers. The purpose of literature was to lead readers to think what the leadership determined was best that they think" (Hockx 65). Accordingly, on the one hand, this system leaves little room of agency to officials if they are to obey the regulation; on the other hand, if the officials do see the significance of creativity and freedom in the process of making art, there's the possibility of great cultural products made with the support of these officials.

The time when Wu was in office is acutely the time when political capital plays a vital role in the modern Chinese field (Hockx 52). Between 1974 and 1976, at the very end of Chinese Cultural Revolution, Wu Tianming studied directing at Beijing Film College. In October 1983, seven years after the "official" ending of Cultural Revolution, Wu was appointed as head of Xi'an Film Studio after being a log keeper and assistant director there. Particularly, the relationship between art making and politics in the post-cultural revolution period can be understood in a twofold way. One is the state's oppression on the autonomy of what to create and produce, with a strict direction of political propaganda and ideology. The other is its strict control on financial support: the financial determining power the government has over cultural production. As Michel Hockx pointed out: "the pure literary field of the 1980s and all its seemingly autonomous literary values was in fact a state-sponsored system; and in order to obtain more autonomy from the state, and from the market, the Chinese literary field should adopt a version of the ruling party's ideology. This would allow it to gather sufficient followers (readers) to break off any latent reliance on state support, while at the same time resisting market pressure" (59). In this case, Hockx asserts that "heteronomy arriving in a field through the producers who are the least capable of succeeding according to the norms it imposes", in which leaves tremendous power on the shoulders of the officials in studios (59). As such, "the literary field can be viewed as 'the economic world reversed' and is influenced by symbolic capital, the opposite of economic capital" (Hockx 59). Nevertheless, even during what was considered the most 'autonomous' period of literary production in contemporary China, one shall note the powerful position of editors, as both beneficiaries of state privileges and cultivators of young writers in search of symbolic capital. Under the system of state censorship, numerous internationally-recognized films are not made public, yet with Wu's protection, they are produced successfully.

Under this condition, Wu Tianming's role as head of Xi'an Film Studio struggles to break free from the boundary and to establish autonomy. As a result, there developed a relative autonomy in how the literary communities could create narratives, and "broaden our perspective beyond the Cold War political dualism and beyond the politicized narrative of 'mainstream' development" (Hockx 60). However, this period of autonomy also reflects certain characteristics of Chinese cinema of that time: the value of a film lies in how it represents China on a global level and how it may contribute to the nation.

Wu's very aware of a balance between the state and the space of autonomy artists needed is reflected in his own writings. During Wu Tianming's administration, he launched a movement of reformation to the desolate Chinese film field. He firmly stated his goal as "transforming the official site of propaganda into an artistic production site" (Yan). With this leading belief in the freedom of art-making, Wu has ensured a relative autonomy for that generation of filmmakers. Wu's staying in power reflects the temporary period of autonomy pointed out by Hockx:

> There is an existing image of the 1980s as an era of tremendously exciting intellectual fermentation, especially in the arts and humanities, and feverish interest in new, experimental forms of artistic expression. On the other hand, in the 1980s the socialist system had not yet been completely dismantled, and this new literary elite not only reaped symbolic profits but also profited from continued state support for writing, publication, and distribution. (58)

As such, Wu Tianming's personal determination and decisions function as key elements in supporting the young generation's artistic creation. This revolution was marked by his generosity and bravery in providing opportunities for young talents, such as the leading directors of the fifth generation, Zhang Yimou, Huang Jianxin, He Ping, Zhou Xiaowen, and Gu

Changwei. Their works are uniquely shot and won fame for Chinese cinema on a global stage. To this extent, Wu's humanist policy has actually created a healthy and carefree production field for young directors. It has been pointed out the severe situation artists faced when the cultural field was largely under "control of material and symbolic capital," it is in doubt whether "the economic logic of maximizing material and symbolic profit exhaust the range of actions and goal that agents pursue in the cultural field" (Hockx 50).

In addition to the relative autonomy Wu Tianming ensured by resisting the oppressive political capital, Wu is wise in economic capital management. Among the sixteen major film studios that's under the management of the Film Bureau, Xi'an Film Studio was the one that did not compromise itself under financial pressures. The directors are able to produce art solely, not too much entangled with political imprints not only because the relative autonomy they are granted by Wu, but also crucially, Wu as the head of the Film Studio gives full financial support to the potentiality of art. When Zhang Yimou tries to shoot *Red Sorghum* (1987), he observed that there were no red sorghums at the place. At that time when the creation of art is required to report to the government first, Wu privately approved this immediately and collected enough money for Zhang to start planting red sorghums so that it can start shooting in time (Wu 18). The act of generosity marks more than Wu's support of art, but his belief in that art should be fully supported, even if at the cost of his own loss financially. When asked about this decision to entrust an inexperienced director to a whole film, he answered: "There's a strength of determination in Zhang's character. A person like this will succeed in doing anything" (Ma 2015). This observation can be supported by the hardships Zhang has endured when acting in *Old Well*. When Wu chose Zhang to be the protagonist of his film *Old Well*, Zhang uses sands to toughen Zhang's hands and back in order to have his skin closer to the character Sun Wangquan. Moreover, in order to act out the realistic hunger and desperation the character has when trapped in the well, he starved himself for three days (Ma, 2015). It is remarked that "only Zhang himself knows that the 'Best Actor' in Tokyo Film Festival was a trade by his life" (Ma, 2015). Wu's full support of the younger generation is also reflected in his impersonal decisions as for how he gives opportunities to the young director from outside to make a film regardless of the old directors who are begging for opportunities in his own studio. He smartly replied to the doubt people had about this: "Those old directors haven't produced good films for so long. But if I give money to the young directors, at least, they will gain experience that will contribute to his later creation" (Ma, 2015).

In addition, the studio head Wu Tianming had his own way of keeping a balance between artistic and commercial movies that allows for a global positioning of modern Chinese films when Chinese literary production took place in the context of a socialist system. In other words, Wu deals with economic capital well when it may affect artistic pursuits. While he fully supported films such as *King of Children* (1987) and *Red Sorghum*, he also let directors produce films such as *The Last Frenzy* (1987) to gain benefits (Yan). Moreover, in order to balance the dynamics of artistic production and consumerist production, he not only encouraged artistic production but also established awards for contribution for those directors.

Collectively, Wu Tianming provides more than simply financial support, but a field of artistic creation that allows for relative autonomy. Hockx noted that "the postcolonial power relations and gender relations" were at work in cultural production as a result of "the relative autonomy of the literary field" (54). This is not only shown through his support of the young inexperienced directors but also his support in the destabilization of social norms in others' and his own films. For example, in Zhang Yimou's *Red Sorghum*, the overthrow of gender is so evident as for how the female takes on the role of a manager, leading the whole group of males. Consequently, how exactly Wu Tianming's own films have benefited from the artistic field he helps initiate and how Wu as a filmmaker contributes to the field artistically are to be furtherly discussed in the next section.

Wu's Artistic Creation in the Chinese Western

As a cultural agent, Wu Tianming's contribution to the field of film production largely lies in his achievement in the Chinese Western, not only through his support of young Chinese directors but also as a stunning, prominent filmmaker himself. Within the artistic field initiated by Wu's administration, political and economic capitals were in upcoming young talents' hands. However, more notably, Wu provided artistic capital by contributing a visual creation that added to the critical formation of the Chinese Western, which of course also blossomed under his wing. Essentially, Wu's role as an official and as a cultural agent has initiated the remarkable achievement of the Chinese Westerns, and his artistic creation has helped its development reach a peak that is represented by Zhang Yimou's *Red Sorghum*. Particularly, two traits have marked the critical role of Wu Tianming: the autonomy he created during his administration as the head of Xi'an Studio and the newly imagined national aesthetics embodied in his Chinese Western genre films, which offer new possibilities to the reconstruction after the nation's history of turmoil. This section analyzes his particular innovation in the formation of the Chinese Western by utilizing a case study of *Old Well*. Through an examination of Wu's representative film *Old Well*, in line with other representative Chinese Westerns, this section argues that the artistic success of the Chinese Western is a result of continuous aesthetics, one of which was created by Wu. Accordingly, Wu Tianming has enacted an age of flourishment in Chinese cinema by pioneering this genre creation of the Chinese Western, which not only deals with the generational question of cultural identity, but also provides answers in the historical confusion of the post-Mao era.

The initiation and rise of the Chinese Western stands at the intersection of a historical outcry for a cultural solution and the individual's intellectual pursuit of a breakthrough. Wu was appointed as head of Xi'an Film Studio in 1983, during a post-revolutionary transitional era marked as a time of aftermath.

In the mid-1980s, the field of cultural production was marked by a cultural fever (*wenhua re*). This cultural fever is "developed as a counter-discourse to the earlier ideological emphasis on class struggle," and "various explorations of broader cultural issues" are brought up with the hope of "better understanding China's past, present, and future" (Kuoshu 214). Zhang Xudong points out that this cultural fever marked the emergence of "a new discursive institution relatively 'autonomous' to state-administered discourse, despite its prematureness and precariousness, between the crushing forces of existing symbolic orders" (72). Shooting films were Wu and his peers' way of exerting this "autonomy" and joining the formation of an alternative discourse. Accordingly, this period of cultural discussion has allowed the "social space" for a cultural debate that has unfolded on a national scale, and with unprecedented ideological as well as theoretical aggressiveness (Zhang 130). Particularly, with this cultural fever, the "root-searching" movement has been a prominent trend among Chinese artists and writers. By searching for their cultural roots, artists and writers as cultural agents deal with the discursively formed past, readdress the embodiment of the present, and look to a promising future. In line with this root-searching trend, a return to left-wing realism in the 1980s in order to look for an answer is also common in the 1980s. Wu's globally-recognized films such as *Life*, *Old Well*, and *King of Masks* all actively engaged with realism in order to construct a national identity. Consequently, besides the intention to look for an alternative identity other than being influenced by the West and at the same time looking for western recognition, cultural productions in the 1980s and 1990s have demonstrated a return to left-wing realism in order to look for an answer. The flourishing of "root-searching" novels also fueled the imagination of filmmaking since the early films made in that period are mostly an adaptation of writers' stories. In this light, the rise of the Chinese Westerns, or Wu's insight in launching the Chinese Westerns, with an emphasis in phenomenal and distinguishing images entitled to a Chineseness, is a filmic search for "root" and the filmmakers cultural response to deal with the historical baggage and look to a promising future.

Consequently, what Wu Tianming faces is not only an intellectual's task to deal with the historical baggage but also a leader's guiding direction of artistic creations and visual imaginaries that can acutely capture the temporality. As a leader, what Wu Tianming has successfully brought to the table is the official guiding policy of an initiation of the Chinese Western. However, the term "Chinese Western" was not coined by Wu, but by the film critic Zhong Dianfei, "who had been a catalyst in renovating Chinese cinematic concepts" (Kuoshu 214). With his suggestion, Xi'an Film Studio's journal was renamed as *Chinese Western*. With this coinage, Wu Tianming demonstrates his desire to have Xi'an film studio "distinguish itself from the others by marketing a new kind of film that would be known as the Chinese Western" (Kuoshu 214). Therefore, the act of initiating the Chinese Western is both nationalistic and iconoclastic: it placed Wu in a position to deny all other existing visual representations and denoted an ambition to redefine Chineseness. To better understand Wu's initiation of the Chinese Western here, it might be helpful to look at Mao's practice of making Marxism Chinese. The Chinese Western, a concept borrowed from American film tradition of the Western, which idealizes the American past of peripatetic cowboys of the 19th century as they explored new frontiers, is constructed as a Chinese version of the rough environment and tough-guy film (Kuoshu 214). Similarly, Mao's practice of "making Marxism Chinese" borrows the Western concept of Marxism and adds Chinese characteristics to it. According to Zhang Xudong, this act of borrowing can be an act of both iconoclasm and nationalism because: "China's immediate past of communist revolution and socialist construction not only stands as a defiant project of working out a society's own possibility nourished in its situation;... it also marks the climax of the absorption of the historical vision (and heritage, so long as Marxism remains a self-critique of the bourgeois history) of the West" (131). In this light, Wu Tianming's promotion of the Chinese Western is also a reflection of what Zhang framed as both a defiant project that looks for the possibility based on its own cultural heritage and a absorption of the historical vision of the West: adopting the features of American Westerns and construct the original traits of Chineseness. At the scene of cultural production, the cry for a new interpretation and new imagination is reflected as a need for a reconstruction of a national subject. Chinese Western has accordingly become the perfect embodiment.

Compared to the American Western, the type of Chinese Western Wu Tianming and his peers initiated was a product of historical turmoil, characterized by a depoliticized image of nature and a tough guy that redefined the Confucian gentleman and celebrated new forms of masculinity. Two features have helped define the creation of Chinese Western: the landscape marked by a reconstruction of national allegory, hidden mysteries and wisdom, and the sexuality marked by iconoclastic gender representation in *Red Sorghum*. The model of American Westerns here is used as a reference for us to better understand the creation of the Chinese Western. Three points are made to understand this new way of dealing with "nature": first, the difference in dealing with nature in American Western and Chinese Western; second, the heterogeneity of this invention of nature in the Chinese Western and how it elucidates Chineseness; third, the new visual imaginary of nature as a national allegory.

First of all, Chinese Westerns distinguish itself from American Westerns in its denotation of nature. Typical American West tends to present nature not as wilderness but as "containing a cultural alternative: The landscape here hides neglected history, legends, and folklore that need to be rediscovered, represented, and used as a mirror for the cultural center in looking at itself" (Esther Yau 1987–88, 33). The iconic image of an American frontier that symbolizes vast freedom and waits for explorations by immigrants is obviously outward. However, what the Chinese Western concerns is a reconsideration of the past, inwardly, in order to make sense of what happened. As Kuoshu points out, whereas in the American West, nature functions as a cultural alternative, the nature in the Chinese Westerns most of the time function as a national allegory (215).

Three Chinese Western films have elucidated this national task endowed in the utilization of the image of nature well. *Yellow Earth* (1984) as the leading film which portrays an Taoist ideal in the connectedness between earth and human in which the "human will thrive if harmonizes with nature" (Kuoshu 215). Nature as a national allegory responds to the cultural fever asking for a solution to deal with the post-revolutionary current and the turbulent past. This take on nature as a national allegory from *Yellow Earth* is even more prominent in *Old Well*. Unlike in *Yellow Earth* where humans need to live a harmonious relationship with nature in order to survive, in *Old Well* nature is portrayed as an evil force objectified as thousands of wells that never provide water: it kills, it dries, it does not leave space for humans to survive. In the meantime, nature is intertwined with the daunting force of history: through generations' efforts, people struggled, fought, and died for it, yet it remains unchanging. This twofold force together weighed heavily on the shoulder of this generation just as the historical task of reconstructing cultural identity was shouldered by that generation of cultural agents. This understanding of the nature-human relationship repetitively is reflected in upcoming films and narratives. This element of an untamed nature is inherited and also peaked in *Red Sorghum*. In *Red Sorghum*, the nature element is transfigured from wildness into mystery and the thickness of sorghum signifies the ambiguity and the obscurity of history (debatably, the scene happened at the *Red Sorghum*, whether or not a scene of rape), whereas the wilderness, where Jiu'er is carried or sold from her own household to the boss, signifies the road to destruction, if followed the way of the feudalistics, or the road to reconstruction, if being captured or interrupted by Jiang Wen.

As nature is utilized to elucidate an alternative narrative about the making of history, we have to note the heterogeneity of this invention in the Chinese Western. Jing Wang noted that the romantic syndrome of the Chinese Western in its subliminal portrayal of nature and landscape "is a manifestation of the displaced historical desire of the cultural subject denied its agency" (215). Consequently, by making nature into a subliminal object one pursues, the film portrays nature as this "allegory of the reconstructed National Subject in search of metaphorical means of empowerment" (Wang Jing 215). As a result, this heterogeneity leads us to focus on the mutual reflection of nature and the man in it so as to construct Chineseness.

Consequently, besides the new imagery of an untamed nature, the other artistic contribution by Wu lies in the gender role: the imagination of a tough guy masculinity. I argue that the reconstruction of a rough guy type that shines over *Red Sorghum* is a continuation of *Old Well*, in which masculinity is portrayed as a subtle combination of both a rough guy and confucian gentleman.

The challenge of a traditional "confucian gentleman" was eminent since the fifth generation's precursory film *One and Eight* (1983). As noted, the traditional configuration of a gentleman is marked by a Confician imagination of a gentle male where "masculine beauty seems to lie more in intelligence and gentility than in physical build and rough manners" (Kuoshu 216). The rise of the Chinese Western shows a tendency of the shift of masculinity to the "rough type," which is often embodied in such unconventional protagonists as thieves, bandits, or murderers according to (Kuoshu 217). For example, in *One and Eight*, the presentation of masculinity emphasizes the rough side by having a group of imprisoned bandits become heroes: they fight Japanese invaders and are willing to die for a higher purpose.

Wu Tianming's *Old Well* continues with this cinematic exploration of masculinity by creating a combination of both roughness and a Confucian gentleness which is reflected in Wangquan's lingering or hesitation between obeying his family's demands or following his own desire. However, the cinematic search for masculinity, when informed by such concepts as individuality, nationality, and resurrection, may often appear male-narcissistic, sexist, violent, and often at the expense of women. Wangquan, the young well-digger in *Old Well*, has the love of two women. Even though in the book *Celluloid China*, *Old Well* is read as a national allegory, Rey Chow argued that it can't because it lacks an external enemy. Conversely, I argue that *Old Well* can still be read as a national allegory because the enemy is the past: what the film narrative in the end tells is how a man, with proper technology and knowledge can overcome history, which is represented in the imagination of nature. At this point, the "cultural root" offered by Wu Tianming is one dug out from both the naturally inherited landscape and a newly imagined masculinity that indulges in roughness.

The visual construction of a rough guy, which was enriched in *Old Well*, peaked in *Red Sorghum*. Zhang Yimou's *Red Sorghum* focuses on a rough-type seasonal worker and how he seduces the new bride of the owner of a wine distillery, rescues her by murdering her leper husband, weds her by showing his body to be stronger than those of the others working at the distillery, wins her back from bandits by courageously challenging their leader, and eventually loses her to Japanese bullets when the workers at the distillery ambush the invaders under his command. Here, the search for masculinity is merged into an allegory of national fate; both masculinity and nationality call for empowerment and revival. The refigured masculinity indicated a gender desire to shed not only its earlier civility in representation but also its weak national-culture status.

In the end, the flourish of the Chinese Western demonstrates the expressive nationalist drive in fifth-generation directors. As director of

Yellow Earth noted: We were working with the idea that life in Shaanbei, the northern region of Shaanxi Province, could be equated to the position that China occupies in the contemporary world. I wanted to express how the Chinese have lived for many, many years. The location is a microcosm. That place is one of the most backward places I know, and China is backward (Kuoshu 220). In fact, a successful figuration of contemporary art can never be separated from a reconsideration of the past/history, just as Wu himself noted: "A person who does not have the courage to admit his/her shortcomings can hardly make any progress; a nation that does not have the courage to admit its defects is doomed" (Zhang J. 43).

Revisioning Wu'S Film Trajectory

A reconsideration of Wu Tianming's contribution to the cultural production in 1980s is telling of what may lead to the flourish of a field: the presence of economic capital, political capital, and symbolic capital. Particularly, an examination of Wu's own film trajectory in light of cultural production can help locate how three capitals are functioning: the making of each film has demonstrated the critical transformation of Chinese cultural production and the success or failure of each can reflect a presence or absence of certain capitals. At the last section, this paper moves on with a brief investigation of Wu's film trajectory as it not only offers a trope into the critical transformation of 20th century in the post-Mao time but also tells more about how an artist's creation is so much entangled with the support of economic, political and symbolic capital. With this investigation, this paper hopes to ask for a reflection on the field of our contemporary filmmaking and an examination of what may be missing.

The flourishing of the Chinese Western identifies the peak of Wu's own filmmaking. As we have analyzed above, Wu's administration in the

1980s has led to the blossom of the Chinese Westerns and reflected his wit in pursuing symbolic capital and economic capital under a field of dominating political capital. Meanwhile, Wu's own film trajectories also turn out to be a vivid illustration of the dynamics of the field of cultural production in the post-cultural production era. Wu's first full-directing film, *River Without Buoys*, was a production in reaction to the political atmosphere of the time. Made in 1984, eight years after the Cultural Revolution, it follows the dominant idea of trying to blame certain "bad" elements in the Party for the historical turmoil instead of a thorough reflection. Wu Tianming knows the system of censorship so well that he strives for creative ways to improvise for his artistic pursuit. In *River Without Buoys*, there's a scene when the protagonist Pan Laowu jumped into the river naked to swim in front of people. In the year of 1984, a time marked by the strong ideological control of the Cultural Revolution, a scene like this would definitely not be permitted to be shown in a public space. Wu has intelligently balanced well with the political capital as to make the scene not a real act of swimming nakedly, but, having Pan Laowu wearing naked-color pants to perform.[①] Then made in the same year, the film *Life* touches upon a specific pain of that generation's young people- the pain of identity, the fixed boundary between city and countryside, which is acutely represented by the imagery of a bridge. These creations of specificities add a vivid note to that time period's artistic creation and how autonomy is made out of creativity. Altogether these form a picture of how an artist strives to expand the boundaries forced upon artistic creation, to battle political capital, and to feed artistic desire with small, delicate, and creative moves.

Afterwards, Wu's film *Old Well* demonstrates a successful model at the scene of cultural production. Wu's directing peaks at the making of *Old Well*.

---

① This is noted by Prof. Ye Tan in a seminar dedicated to Wu Tianming and Chinese cinema at the University of South Carolina in 2018.

Rey Chow has read *Old Well* as a national allegory in terms of its pursuit in questing the Western technology without being influenced by the ideology of the West, which relates to the global trend of searching for a universality. However, as Hockx asserted, before the 1980s, Chinese cultural production did not "choose to sideline with the participation in the global literary world," whereas the opening of the New Era in economics leads the whole society into a stage of gaining western recognition, which undoubtedly influenced the cultural production (53). The making of Old Well nevertheless falls into the category of filmmaking that wishes to find an alternative narrative of prosperity yet still looks for a western recognition. Accordingly, the 1980s indicates a turn in Chinese cultural production in which if there's an intention of gaining western recognition. Therefore, with this artistic capital, and the economic and political capitals that are allowed under his administration, *Old Well* turns out to be one of Wu's most successful films.

However, Wu's artistic creation came to a halt when Wu was in the US in the early 1990s, along with a halt to his official life. Of the five years Wu stayed in the US, Chinese cinema went through a critical transformation that is marked by Chen Kaige and Zhang Yimou's peak film production with *Farewell my Concubine* (1993) and *To Live* (1994). Later, however, in the years after Wu Tianming came back to China, Chinese film production has been driven by capital and market. Zhang Yimou started to cooperate with private capital and produced films aimed for entertainment and market, such as *Curse of the Golden Flower* (2006) and *A Woman, a Gun and a Noodle Shop* (2009). When Wu's last film *Song of Phoenix* (2016) was released in China, however, the producer had to kneel in front of the camera to beg the audience to pay attention to this film, an interesting phenomenon that reflects the dominating power of consumerism, capital, market. Though there's also a scholar arguing that one shall not identify Wu Tianming as the Master in *Song of Phoenix* Master in terms of how much Wu has achieved and how the final films still provide an alternative perspective to the rising consumerism

(Wang Jie, 92). Of course, one should note *Song of Phoenix* was fighting against the power of the market that's too hard to beat:

> When the socialist system was gradually phased out in the 1980s and replaced by a market-driven system under state control, this meant that the primary function of literature was no longer propaganda. Psychological control of writers, however, remained in place, albeit in an ever more relaxed form. As a result, the "private calculation" of political risks was more and more often balanced by calculations of potential economic and symbolic gains. (Hockx, 81)

Nevertheless, After Wu Tianming came back from the US, he offered one of the last applauded films in his career as an artist: *The King of Masks* (1995). In a very well-organized narrative, the director offers us a journey of the oppression of patriarchal society, the pain of female gender, the decency of artists, the power domination of the official system, and as always, the sublimity of humanity. However, after that, Wu's films are also challenged by the market. As Michael Hockx suggested, "The relationship between literature and politics while they are united in their dismissal of market-driven literary production" (52). The film *CEO* (2002) just reflected how at first Wu's film was unavoidably imprinted with political elements while the reception of *Song of Phoenix* in the Chinese market reflects the new age Chinese film market is highly driven by consumerism and entertainment. One can read it as an outcry of a traditional artist that has gone through an age of planned economy in China but was struck by the trend of globalization and the rise of consumerism.

In the final years of Wu Tianming's film production, he's more concerned with the Chinese identity, challenged by globalization and westernization. Thus, we can see strong nationalism represented in *CEO* and *An Unusual Love*, and the insistence on the tradition in *King of Masks* and *Song of Phoenix*. In the film *CEO,* we are confronted by the "advanced West" in terms of technology from Germany. In *An Unusual Love,* we see the overwhelming powerlessness of the human body in light of diseases. In both films, Wu Tianming offers his perspective on China's reaction to this challenge. In *CEO*, it is by adopting the technology of the West, relying on a proper localization and the "will" and hard work of Chinese people. Success ultimately relies on the Chinese people. In *An Unusual Love*, when the western medical system gives up the protagonist, it is by the belief of the Chinese traditional medical system and its cooperation with the Western medicine, that the protagonist is able to regain life. Moreover, King of Masks also deals with this self-positioning of China on this global stage and the positioning of Chinese tradition. *The King of Masks* was challenged by the severe reality that he himself doesn't have a son and the tradition required that the heir had to be a male. When a famous male opera star tries to hire the Master, he rejects it because that star plays femininity in operas. As we know, the Master "comes from a long tradition of street persons and he doesn't want to change" (Maslin). In the end, the Master accepted the little girl as his heir. We can read this as the insistence in traditional art, its inheritance is more important than the rules and the boundaries associated with this tradition. Thus, the insistence on tradition is reconciled with the particular constraints of the time, regardless of gender or family ties. In terms of thinking about the penetration of nationalism, it is important to note that, these films are nonetheless also a product of "cultural works that are produced in objective historical situations and institutional frameworks by agents using different strategies and following different trajectories in the field," thus, "the reception of such works also takes place in specific historically constituted situations" (Bourdieu 1993). Just like how Chen Kaige confessed that "he and the 152 other students who entered the Film Academy in 1978 shared a profound contempt for the cinema they had grown up with [the Communist cinema]", which unavoidably has affected his filmmaking (Berry 2012). It will be unfair to judge those films' achievements solely based on today's aesthetic ideas, ignorant of what are the situations that produced it.

Today, when one thinks of early Chinese cinema, one would unavoidably think of *Yellow Earth*, *Red Sorghum*, *Life* and *Old Well*, Zhang Yimou, and Chen Kaige. However, of these connections, one can never neglect Wu Tianming, the significant figure who not only produced groundbreaking films but also set the ground for the globally-famous Chinese filmmakers. By analyzing the dynamics of the cultural production field in the 1980s in light of the critical three capitals, we may note what is missing in today's cultural production. In the 1980s, when the conceptions of the past are challenged and waiting to be redefined and represented, Wu has helped and participated in the artistic blossom by battling the political capital, providing economic capital, and contributing artistic capital to the field himself- all three critical to form a healthy field. Last but not least, underlying all these achievements, what remains unforgettable is the director's true aspiration for art and humanity. Wu's humanistic character continues to shine through his achievements and contributions besides his artistic creation. When he won the "Academy Honorary Award" in 2005, he donated the reward to the village where he shot *Old Well*: "I want to donate the money to Laojing Village. The two-hundred-year-old well went dry there. I hope the money can help them dig a new well of clean water" (Wu 2014). As a whole, Wu Tianming as a filmmaker still asks for way more research than he has received today, so we may peek into the once glorious moments of Chinese cultural production.

Works Cited:

Berry, Chris. *Chinese Cinema*. Routledge, 2012.

Bian lian 变脸 (The King of Masks). Directed by Wu Tianming, Beijing Youth Film Studio, 1996.

Bai niao chao feng 百鸟朝凤 (Song of the Phoenix). Directed by Wu Tianming, Beijing Laurel Films, 2016.

Bourdieu, Pierre. *Outline of a Theory of Practice*. 25. printing, Cambridge Univ. Press, 2010.

Chen, Xihe 陈犀禾 , and Wang, Yanyun 王艳云 . "Wu Tianming yu yige shidai de zhongguo dianying" 吴天明与一个时代的中国电影 [J] [Wu Tianming and Chinese Cinema]. Dianying yishu 电影艺术 , 2016 (04):139–144.

Feichang aiqing 非常爱情 (An Unusual Love). Directed by Wu Tianming, Beijing Film Studio, 1999.

Hockx, Michel. "The Literary Field and the Field of Power: The Case of Modern China." Paragraph, vol. 35, no. 1, Mar. 2012, pp. 49–65. Edinburgh University Press Journals, doi:10.3366/para.2012.0041.

Hockx, Michel, and Ivo Smits, editors. *Reading East Asian Writing: The Limits of Literary Theory*. Routledge Curzon, 2003.

Hong gaoliang 红 高 粱 (Red Sorghum). Directed by Zhang Yimou, Xi'an Film Studio, 1988.

Huang tudi 黄土地 (Yellow Earth). Directed by Chen Kaige, Guangxi Film Studio, 1984.

Jia-Xuan, Zhang. *Film Quarterly*, vol. 42, no. 3, 1989, pp. 41–43. *JSTOR*, www. jstor. org/stable/1212602. Accessed 31 Jan. 2020.

Janet Maslin, *Bridging Loneliness, Despite the disguises*. The New York Times, Wednesday, April 28, 1999.

Kuoshu, H. H. *Celluloid China: Cinematic Encounters with Culture and Society*. Southern Illinois University Press, 2002.

Lao Jing 老井 (Old Well). Directed by Wu Tianming, Xi'an Film Studio, 1987.

Lim, Song. Hwee, and Julian, Ward. *The Chinese Cinema Book*. Bloomsbury Publishing, 2020.

Ma, Ting 马婷 . "Lishi fengyun yu chuangxin yinxiang xi'an dianying zhipian chang yingye fazhan yanjiu" 历史风云与创新映像西安电影制片厂影业发展研究（1979–2000）[D][The Historical Dynamics and Innovations of Xi'an Film Studio]. 上海大学 , 2015.

Meiyou hangbiao de heliu 没有航标的河流 (River Without Buoys). Directed by Wu Tianming, Xi'an Film Studio, 1983.

Rensheng 人生 (Life). Directed by Wu Tianming, Xi'an Film Studio, 1984.

Shouxi zhixing guan 首席执行官 (CEO). Directed by Wu Tianming, Beijing Film Studio, 2002.

Wang, Jie 王杰 . "Wu Tianming bushi nage chui suona de ren" 吴天明不是那个 " 吹唢呐的人 "[J][Wu Tianming is not the person who plays suona] . Shanghai yishu pinglun 上海艺术评论 ,2016(04):92–93.

Wang, Jing. High Culture Fever: Politics, Aesthetics, and Ideology in Deng's China. Berkeley: University of California Press, c1996 1996. http://ark. cdlib. org/ark:/13030/ft0489n683/.

"Wu Tianming jianli ji zuoping nianbiao" 吴天明简历及作品年表 [J]. Dangdai dianying 当代电影 , 2003 (01): 58.

Yau, Esther C. M. 1987–1988. "*Yellow Earth*: Western Analysis and a Non-Western Text." *Film Quarterly* 41.2: 22–23.

Yan, Liang 颜亮 . "Kengqiang niandai: Wu Tianming yu xiyingchang de naxie nian" 铿锵年代：吴天明与西影厂的那些年 [Wu Tianming and Xi'an Film Studio]. http://ent. sina. com. cn/m/c/2014-03-14/01004111134. shtml. 2013. Accessed 8 Apr. 2018.

Zhang, Xudong. *Chinese Modernism in the Era of Reforms: Cultural Fever, Avant-Garde Fiction, and the New Chinese Cinema*. Duke University Press, 1997.

Soviet Schooling: The Case of Joseph Brodsky

Daria Smirnova*

中文摘要 本文作者以俄裔美籍诗人约瑟夫·布罗茨基的作品和思想为据，论述了苏联教育体制中存在的一些问题。布罗茨基在《小于一》这部作品集中通过回忆他童年时期的校园生活对苏联的教育体制进行反思和批评，认为这种教育丧失了教育的基本属性。布罗茨基还提出这种教育类似无所不在的宣传，容易引发福柯主义层面上的反抗，而这种反抗又是自然的、潜意识的和不可避免的。作者总结说，苏联这种充斥着文艺和视觉宣传的教育会逐渐引发人们的冷漠，并最终对它们所传达的信息产生厌倦。苏联许多学生排斥这种教育模式，这也是布罗茨基文章产生广泛影响的原因。

关键词 教育；约瑟夫·布罗茨基;《小于一》

In his work *Nations and Nationalism* Ernest Gellner points out the importance of a wide spread education system in state-formation. He believes that industrial society with its idea of statehood "can only be achieved by a

---

* 作者为俄罗斯人，美国南卡罗莱纳大学比较文学专业在读博士生，主要从事跨学科研究。

fairly monolithic education system" (134). This education should be diffused through an entire population, not tied to faith or church. Such state-run universal training helps the state to maintain a unitary culture and communication style, which "monopolizes legitimate culture almost as much as it does legitimate violence, or perhaps more so" (134). Education, Gellner believes, produces a shared high culture that is "the minimal shared atmosphere, within which alone the members of the society can breathe and survive and produce" (36). In other words, in an industrial society, one cannot survive outside the prevailing culture as it functions as a scaffolding structure of the given society. "[…] a modern industrial state can only function with a mobile, literate, culturally standardized, interchangeable population" (44). In this sense, fungibility is not a diminishing feature, rather a characteristic of belonging that, along with responsibilities, yields plenty of privileges for a citizen.

Benedict Anderson approaches the formation of the idea of a nation from a different angle that nonetheless compliments Gellner's ideas. He asserts that the advent of newspapers and novels changed the perception of time by introducing the notion of simultaneity. Anderson claims: "The idea of sociological organism moving calendrically through homogeneous, empty time is a precise analogue of idea nation, which also is conceived as a solid community moving steadily down (or up) history" (26). While the author does not claim that newspapers and novels created nations, he, as Jonathan Culler puts it, makes it clear that "the novel was a condition of possibility for imagining something like a nation" (49).

The notion of simultaneity that, according to Anderson, the novel reinforces, helps to create unity—something the Soviet government was trying to achieve. However, if it is pushed further, this concept can also help those in the resistance to consolidate and obtain a sense of being a part of what I call "imagine opposition"—an understanding that even though one would never meet (or meet but not openly discuss politics with them) everyone who has similar objections to the regime, such people create community. The abstract idea that there are others who disagree to the same level and at the same time as one, can reinforce and encourage resistance. It is fair to assume that this is how at some point the Soviet school system backlashed.

The Soviet education system is an example of how the newly-formed state utilized schools to first create a nation and secondly maintain its ideological credibility and, at the same time, how it fails in doing so. As a multi-national country, the USSR had to offer a school system that would define its national subjectivity as a unified nation. In addition, taking into consideration Anderson's idea on the role of the novel, it is worthwhile to look not only at the school system in general, but also at its literature school program in particular, and how it changed throughout the years and what objectives it set.

Another reason as to why it is crucial to examine literature curricular closely is the attitude towards the written word in Russia. Russia has an uncommon long-standing tradition of perceiving poets as prophets who are responsible to tell the nation what they are, where to go and what do to. This dates to the 19th century when both Alexander Pushkin (1828) and Mikhail Lermontov (1841) wrote their *The Prophet* poems. With the pervasiveness of state oppression—during the Tsarist times censorship and pro-monarchy propaganda were very powerful as well—literature was viewed as the last stronghold of impartiality: the tighter the government tried to control literature, the more trustworthy is was becoming in the eye of the reader. This idea gained a special significance during the Soviet times, which turned *samizdat*[①] into such a crucial phenomenon. Similar to the Tsarist times, Soviet authors were expected to tell the truth and to be ready to be held responsible for their candid texts. Vladimir Bukovsky famously wrote: samizdat is when "I

---

① Or young characters like Pavlik Morozov, who denounced his parents and became part of Soviet mythology as a great hero for being so devout to the state.

write it myself, edit it myself, censor it myself, publish it myself, distribute it myself, and spend jail time for it myself'. The goal of samizdat was to serve as "political and cultural opposition to official attempts to create Homo Soveticus - the perfect Soviet citizen" (Hurst 5). Those authors believed in their ability to do that precisely because literature and authors were regarded so highly. In 1965, Soviet poet Evgeni Evtushenko wrote a stanza that became and still is acclaimed:

> The poet in Russia is more than a poet.
> Only those in whom the proud spirit of citizenship roams,
> Who find no comfort or peace,
> Are fated to be born as poets in Russia.

Thus, the power of literature that Anderson points out is highlighted in the Russian context by the notion of the writer as a sacred, highly moral, fearless and wise figure who possesses the truth. That explains the pathological fear of the dissident writers that the Soviet government had and the desire to control the school curricular.

Throughout Soviet history, the school canon was in the process of becoming fixed and at the same time was constantly being changed, which indicates both the uncertainty regarding how to achieve the inculcation in the most efficient way and the volatility of the political ideology from one decade to another. The school literature programs from different time periods this paper focuses on—1921, 1938, and 1960—reflect the processes the country was undergoing and the changes in literature and the educational system in general.

In the early 1920s, the War Communism era was coming to an end and was gradually replaced by the New Economic Policy. The new government viewed education as a state priority. Therefore, in 1918 it issued the *Uniform Labor School Regulations*. Under its policies everyone was guaranteed the right to a free secular education—in contrast to the heavily religious school system in Tsarist Russia. However, because of the recent Civil War the implementation of these policies did not start up until 1921, when the first standardized program was developed.

The literature part of the program was influenced by the ideas on education that had been circulating back in 1916–1917 at the First Russian Conference for teachers of Russian and Literature. The approach was distinguished for its attention to providing students with various school programs that they would find satisfying, and for taking students' interests into consideration. The basis of this program was the classical Russian literature of the 19th century—Dostoevsky, Tolstoy, Chekhov, and Turgenev (Ponamorev) Literary texts of earlier periods were generally omitted along with recently emerging Soviet literature and the emergence of socialist realism.

The goal of this list of the texts was to teach students to comprehend literature on an emotional level. Students were expected to read the primary texts before becoming familiar with a theoretical framework or an author's biography (Dobrenko). Such an approach, however, could not survive for long in such circumstances, when everything, especially the arts, was above all supposed to serve the state and inevitably turn into propaganda.

Therefore, the next school program adopted in of 1938 was drastically different. By then the goal of all sciences, arts and culture was building an uber-industrial and hyper-militarized society. During this and two following decades, teachers had fewer and fewer opportunities to change the program (Ponamorev). Last year of high school students were to read plenty of texts on Revolution or about revolutionary ideas and how they were depicted in literature. Clearly, only certain texts, presenting Revolution in a certain light were considered appropriate. Dostoevsky started being considered "too suspicious" and even Russian classics like Tolstoy were interpreted as though they sought socialist Revolution (hence, *Anna Karenina* was not studied while *War and Peace* was presented as a book on patriotism). Many of the Soviet authors from that time, except for the names like Maxim Gorky, Vladimir Mayakovsky, and Alexander Blok, became forgotten as their only value was in being hyperbolically socialist.

The program was meticulously specific not only about what texts pupils would read, but also about how to interpret each work and how to apply the Marxist theory to each text. Textbooks and teachers were viewed as the only ones who had authoritative opinions and students were not encouraged to practice critical thinking. Instead, they were expected to memorize significant parts of texts and analysis, without much reflection. The lists of the excerpts that were supposed to be memorized were also strictly regulated.

Predictably, literary works were selected not necessarily for their artistic value, but chiefly for their capacity to align with the Soviet understanding of the humanities and their role in the Soviet state (Ponamorev). Literary works were counted upon as means of setting examples of heroism—whether military or labor-related—that young Soviet citizens could imitate①. From the mid-1930s to 1960s, school became a place that oppressed creativity and critical thinking while teachers played a role of indoctrinating mediators between the students and the state. As Catriona Kelly observes: "…From 1936 a direct association began to be drawn between literary analysis and the expression of national pride" (535).

The following quote from a standardized school program, grades 6 through 10, 1938, echoes this idea:

> To reveal the grandeur of the classical Russian literature that many generations of revolutionary warriors were brought up on, the enormous principled distinction as well as the moral and political depth of Soviet literature, to teach students to understand the basic stages of literary

① Or young characters like Pavlik Morozov, who denounced his parents and became part of Soviet mythology as a great hero for being so devout to the state.

development, without oversimplification, without schematizing—that was the course's historico-literary objective (challenge/task) in middle school, grades eight through ten.

Soviet literary education in school, although including dozens of good books, was aimed at creating obedient citizens that would have memorized the "ideologically correct" interpretations of the selected works. Felicity Ann O'Dell summarizes some of the myths that were taught through literature classes in the USSR:

- Soviet society is the most democratic, just, humane, productive and non-exploitative in the world, because it lacks class contradictions.
- The Party (as we know it today) is the Party of Lenin. It embodies the precepts of "the most humane of men".
- Society is in a process of transition from socialism to Communism and a united effort will soon bring Communism to the Soviet Union.

It should also be added that the entire history of literature was also viewed as anticipating Socialist revolution. Hence, the interpretation of most texts, if needed, could be adjusted and appropriated for the objectives of socialist education.

After Stalin's death scholars and teachers awaited changes that would foster critical thinking and give more room for various interpretations. Nevertheless, the new school program of 1960 came as a disappointment. It required covering more material in less time, the approach was still dry and too systematic and the only permitted theoretical approaches were Marxism and some historicism. Imbuing ideologically correct notions was still regarded as the chief goal of literature. To be sure, as Kelly notes "Some teachers tried to run literary societies where pupils would read and discuss books not on the syllabus, such as Dostoevsky and Bulgakov" (498), but these attempts were sporadic and for obvious reasons dangerous.

Such was school in the USSR. Highly political, ideological with a focus not on the individual ethics but on shaping the politically correct collectivist mentality. After Stalin's death, however, these socialist ideas, being over-stressed and losing their relevance, helped a generation rich of dissidents to emerge. A number of them expressed their disagreement through literature. One of the most prominent voices of that time was Joseph Brodsky.

Joseph Brodsky, a native of what was then named Leningrad, USSR, is an essayist and a poet of a unique sort. He is, in a sense, a successor of the Silver Age of Russian poetry, and this is especially evident, given his friendship with the famous poet Anna Akhmatova. On the other hand, Brodsky's works stand out from the collections of earlier writers both in style and subject. In 1972, Brodsky was forced by the Soviet government to emigrate, and, after changing places for a while, he settled down in the USA, where he became a professor. Throughout his life in the United States, he taught at several American universities, including Yale, Columbia and Michigan. The poet mastered the English language and translated his own works from Russian into English. He began writing essays primarily in English, while continuing to write poetry in his native tongue. In 1987 Brodsky received a Nobel Prize in literature for his "all-embracing authorship, imbued with clarity of thought and poetic intensity," and in 1991, he was appointed a United States Poet Laureate.

In his essay "Less that One," Brodsky reminisces about the years of his childhood and adolescence that he spent in his native country. This piece can be read as both nostalgic and reprimanding. Brodsky's childhood in a city that was tremendously wounded during the war, was in many ways shaped by the city itself. The regime, and anti-Semitism (Brodsky was Jewish) made his life harder, and for the young boy this hardship was concentrated in an education system that sought to indoctrinate good Soviet citizens and was permeated with anti-Semitic ideas. In the essay the poet goes as far as to compare his school teachers with prison guards. Brodsky had every reason to hate his school experience since from the very young age he realized that Soviet education played a significant role in the state propaganda machine and was employed to inculcate ideologically correct beliefs in the younger generation so as to help the state maintain its power.

In his essay, Joseph Brodsky castigates the school system in Soviet Russia. He claims that school, which he defines as "a factory is a poem is a prison is academia is boredom, with flashes of panic"—taught him not patriotism but what he calls "the art of detachment". For example, he ridicules the ubiquity of Lenin's portraits: "I began to despise even when I was in the first grade … because of his omnipresent images which plagued almost every textbook, every class wall, postage stamps, money, and what not, depicting the man at various ages and stages of his life". He concludes by saying: "I think that coming to ignore those pictures was my first lesson in switching off, my first attempt at estrangement…Anything that bore a suggestion of repetitiveness became compromised and subject to removal. In a way, I am grateful to Lenin. Whatever there was in plenitude I immediately regarded as some sort of propaganda." It follows that, according to Brodsky, such omnipresent propaganda automatically created resistance in a Foucauldian sense, meaning that it was there as a natural, subconscious and inevitable response to the power of the State.

The content of the textbook and the lecture was just as tediously dull as the school environment itself. School buildings were supposed to induce no creative or critical thinking: "On the inside … Soviet school were—at best—sparely functional to the point of bleakness. Some relief to the eye was provided by political symbols—portraits of Lenin and Stalin certainly did hang in prominent places, such as the main staircase" (Kelly, 505). Brodsky reiterates this idea: "[there] were not colors themselves but hints of colors, which might be interrupted only by alternating patches of brown: doors … And through the half-open door you could see another room with the same distribution of gray and white marked by the blue stripe. Plus, a portrait of Lenin and a world map." The only outlet for creativity was vandalism and as Kelly asserts it was a constant problem. Therefore, like the pervasiveness of visual propaganda backfired and made students aloof, so that they became immune to it, the intentional bleakness of interiors and the suppression of creativity led to students expressing themselves via banned artistic forms. Non-socialist realist literature was considered just as vandalistic as graffiti.

The school system as a whole was preoccupied with turning pupils into obedient citizens. Kelly obverses that "Class hours' consistent of sessions not only of 'self-criticism' and of affirmatory discourse: the celebration of Soviet heroes and festivals, the laudatory citation of record-breaking industrial and agricultural statistics, tributes to Party leaders, and so on" (545). O'Dell also claims that: "A sense of social commitment can be described as the fundamental personality characteristic of the model Soviet personality. It comprises a valuing of the interests of the collective over those of the self—or of individuals generally" (33). Thus, it was aimed, using Brodsky's term, at making one feel "less than one"; the state was supposed to be presented as the grand narrative that can survive without an individual, but where this individual's subjectivity would only occur within the boundaries of the state's domain. In other words, paraphrasing Brodsky, in a collectivist society, one could only be either less than one, or more than one.

The poet also notes that "after [school] years [students] ended up with a willpower in no way superior to a seaweed's. Obedience would become both first and second nature." This obedience, however, was an exterior defense mechanism. While students mastered how to compline with the absurd rules and echoes ideologically correct interpretations of the literary texts, they were, during Brodsky's generation, develop a sense of defiance.

Kelly observes, that all this systematic indoctrination had a flip side to it, which the official institutions could not control. That would manifest through a certain skepticism that the propaganda ubiquity provoked in students (568). Brodsky means something similar when he writes: "we entered schools, and whatever elevated rubbish we were taught there, the suffering and poverty were visible all around. You cannot cover a ruin with a page of *Pravda*①". The discrepancy between reality and socialist-realist literature was becoming more and more obvious and that in turn engendered apathy with which students would perceive school material.

Another sphere where Brodsky finds escape from the established brainwashing and which shapes his individual creative voice is the city itself. His discovers relief from the limited Soviet culture in the architecture of St. Petersburg, the city that was planned and built as an epitome of "world culture." He writes in "Less than One": I must say that from these facades and porticoes … I have learned more about the history of our world than I subsequently have from any book. Greece, Rome, Egypt—all of them were there…" and "from the gray, reflecting river flowing down to the Baltic, with an occasional tugboat in the midst of it struggling against the current, I have learned more about infinity and stoicism than from mathematics and Zeno."

The poet believes that it is the system that helped him to become the person he is and allowed the discovery of his creative voice. He goes as far as to call his generation "the most bookish in the history of Russia." He stresses the importance of views on literature had on relationships people would have among his peers and points out that it was literature, not the state, that people were willing to sacrifice for. What emerged as a means for escapism became an integral part of their identity, but this subjectivity was not about belonging to a nation, as the government hoped, rather it was of feeling connection to what they called "world culture", which, according to them, was bigger than

---

① Pravda, (Russian: "Truth") newspaper that was the official organ of the Communist Party of the Soviet Union from 1918 to 1991 (www. britannica. com).

anything Soviet ideology could offer.

Ernest Gellner points out the importance of universal education for allowing social mobility. In such a society, being literate becomes a pre-condition for any other specialisms and occupations stop being hereditary, like it was in agrarian states. High culture that is now available to everyone through the means of schooling starts to define industrial society and needs to be maintained by sustaining universal education system. "Modern man", Gellner states, "is not loyal to a monarch or land or a faith, whatever he may say, but to a culture" (35). The Soviet universal school system—the higher education was also made universal, but it is out of scope of this paper—employed education as a nation-formation tool. Soviet nationalism brought by the permeation of high culture created homogeneity (or a semblance of such) within a closed multiethnic country.

Reasonably, the humanities played a significant role in utilizing education for the state purposes. By taking under control not only school curricular but the ways it had to be implemented, the state paid special attention to literature and history classes as a platform for indoctrination. Even today, most Russians who were schoolers during the Soviet era, can recite same texts regardless of which part of the post-Soviet area they are from. Benedict Anderson asserts that the notion of simultaneity that reading newspapers and novels engendered, made it possible to conceive and realize otherwise a rather elusive idea of nation. In the context of Soviet Russia, however, this worked both ways: while reading same texts enhanced unity among the population, it created a mental domain for resistance. *Samizdat* was one of the means by which authors were voicing their dissidence.

Universal education saturated by literary and visual propaganda was evoking aloofness and eventually immunity for its messages. Demand for absolute obedience with no space for creativity developed in many students outwardly detachment while helping them find deeper connection with others who shared similar nonconformist ideas. Joseph Brodsky's essay is an example of how this process was becoming more substantial after Stalin's death.

Works Cited:

Anderson, Benedict. *Imagined Communities: Reflections on the Origin and Spread of Nationalism*. London: Verso, 2016.

Brodsky, Joseph. *Less Than One: Selected Essays*. London: Penguin Books, 2011.

Culler, Jonathan D. "Anderson and the Novel." *Diacritics*, vol 29, no. 4, 1999, pp. 20–39.

Dobrenko, Eugeny. *Formovka sovetskogo cheloveka.* Akademichesky proekt Press, 1997.

Gellner, Ernest, and John Breuilly. *Nations and Nationalism*. Malden, Mass: Blackwell Publishing, 2013.

Hurst, Mark. *British Human Rights Organizations and Soviet Dissent, 1965–1985*, 2016. Internet resource.

Kelly, Catriona. *Children's World: Growing Up in Russia, 1890–1991*, 2007.

O'Dell, Felicity. *Socialisation Through Children's Literature: The Soviet Example*. Cambridge: Cambridge Univ. Press, 2010.

Ponomarev, Eugeny. "Литература в Советской Школе Как Идеология Повседневности." НЛО, Mar. 2017, magazines. russ. ru/nlo/2017/3/literatura-v-sovetskoj-shkole-kak-ideologiya-povsednevnosti. html.

Volkov, Vladimir. "World Socialist Web Site." *World Socialist Web Site*, 3 May 2017, www. wsws. org/en/articles/2017/05/03/yevt-m03.html.

侨易学视域下的中美文学交流

姜智芹[*]

Abstract Qiao-Yiology is a concept put forward by professor Ye Jun in recent years, which emphasizes relevance, interdisciplinarity and changeability. Qiao-Yiology is devoted to exploring the relationship between different cultures and the general law of human civilization. Qiao-Yiology and the literary exchanges between China and the United States are mutually beneficial, with the former's unique philosophical perspective providing a methodological guidance for the latter, while the latter's affluent experience providing a solid empirical ground for the former.

Keywords Qiao-Yiology; changeability; constancy; literary exchanges between China and the United States

侨易学是近年来叶隽教授提出的观念，它“既是一种理论，一种哲学，同时也是一个领域，一种新兴的学科”，其核心内容在于“探讨异文化间相互关系以及人类文明结构形成的总体规律”。[①] 作为一种理论和

---

* 作者为山东师范大学文学院教授，博士生导师，主要研究方向为欧美文学、中西文学比较。

① 叶隽:《侨易学的观念》,《教育学报》2011 年第 2 期。

方法论，侨易学不仅具有宽阔的哲理思维空间，而且具有实用性和可操作性，本文尝试从侨易学视角对中美文学交流史做一分析和探讨。

由钱林森、周宁主编，周宁、朱徽、贺昌盛、周云龙共同执笔的《中外文学交流史：中国—美国卷》（山东教育出版社，2016年）融汇了多位学者的学识与智慧，对中美文学关系做出了极为详尽的梳理、分析与剖解。用侨易学的理论观照之，可以发现二者之间体现出一种互相印证、互相阐发的关系。

在叶隽看来，侨易学的基本理念是因“侨”致“易”，“这其中既包括物质位移、精神漫游所造成的个体思想观念的形成与创生……也包括不同的文化子系统如何相互作用与精神变形”[①],而在“易”的若干含义中，既有对变化一面的强调，也有对“‘不易’的一面，也就是恒常的一面”[②]的注重。基于以上理论阐释，我们从“异质文学激荡中的变创”“异国形象塑造中的恒常”“侨易个体位移中的观念创生”三个方面，统照中美文学在交流中所带来的文学流派的生成、文学观念的更新以及形象嬗变中的恒常。

一　异质文学激荡中的变创

侨易学概念虽然兼顾变易、简易的研究，但核心部分放在“交易”层面。也就是探讨如何通过“异质相交”而导致发生“精神层面的质性变易”，研究侨易对象发生运动的途径——“地理位置的移动”和“思想文化的流动”。[③]这种“移动”和“流动”是双向的，是相互渗透、相互影响的交互作用。中美诗歌和戏剧（曲）的“侨动”带来的质性发展提供了不同文化子系统如何“相互作用与精神变形”的极好例证。

首先，中国古典诗歌触发美国诗人埃兹拉·庞德发起意象派诗歌

---

① 叶隽:《变创与渐常：侨易学的概念》，北京大学出版社2014年版，第19–20页。
② 叶隽:《变创与渐常：侨易学的概念》，北京大学出版社2014年版，第20页。
③ 叶隽:《变创与渐常：侨易学的概念》，北京大学出版社2014年版，第17页。

运动，开创了美国现代派诗歌的先河。庞德年轻时开始接触中国古典诗歌，翻译了《中庸》《大学》《论语》《诗经》等中国典籍，影响最大的《神州集》被誉为庞德对英语诗歌“最为持久的贡献”和“英语诗歌的经典作品”。[①]庞德十分喜欢中国古典诗歌尤其是李白、杜甫、白居易、王维等人的诗篇中那些画面感很强的描写，认为某些汉字本身就是一幅图画，一个意象，营造出优美的意境。当代英国理论家苏珊·巴斯奈特认为诗歌就像植物的种子，可以通过翻译移植到新的土壤里去，催生出新的植物来。庞德正是从美国的东方文学艺术研究专家欧·费诺罗萨“留下的大批逐字直译汉诗的粗略译文和韦利等的汉诗英译选集中”发现了创新的灵感，“并将其移植到欧美诗坛这块异域土地上，使中国古诗在思想内容和艺术手法等方面对美国和西方的文学艺术及社会生活产生影响，而英美意象派诗歌正可视为从汉诗种子中催生出来的新生植物”，[②]对美国现代诗歌的发展起到了重要作用。

其次，美国意象派诗歌在从中国古诗中获得启迪的同时，“又给予中国新诗以很多启示，帮助催生了中国白话新诗”。[③]作为“诗界革命”的领袖之一，胡适具有开新诗风气之功，而这和他在美国留学（1910–1917）期间对意象派诗歌的接触有很大关系。1913 年 3 月，美国《诗刊》刊发“意象派宣言”，强调运用意象的重要性，主张“意象并置”，避免含混、抽象的议论。时在美国留学的胡适立即产生共鸣，认为这一诗派的观点和自己的主张颇有相似之处，并于 1919 年发表了《论新诗》一文，成为中国新诗的纲领性文件。文中对新诗要有“鲜明扑人的影像”“形式要自由”[④]的理论阐释，体现了他所受到的“意象派宣言”的影响。此后他在意象派诗歌的影响下不仅发表了《文学改良刍议》，还

---

① 赵毅衡:《意象派与中国古典诗歌》,《外国文学研究》1979 年第 4 期。

② 周宁、朱徽、贺昌盛、周云龙:《中外文学交流史：中国—美国卷》，山东教育出版社 2016 年版，第 106 页。

③ 周宁、朱徽、贺昌盛、周云龙:《中外文学交流史：中国—美国卷》，山东教育出版社 2016 年版，第 100 页。

④ 周宁、朱徽、贺昌盛、周云龙:《中外文学交流史：中国—美国卷》，山东教育出版社 2016 年版，第 100 页。

创作出《鸽子》《蝴蝶》《老鸦》等具有意象派风格的诗作。当时施蛰存主编的《现代》月刊也对美国意象派的主将进行集束式译介，从庞德到洛威尔、杜利特尔、弗莱彻，几乎都有译介和述评。在中国新诗运动中，不仅大力介绍、阐释意象派诗歌理论，还倡导创作中国的意象派诗歌，除胡适外，施蛰存、刘半农、王统照、刘大白、沈尹默等都创作过意象派风格的诗篇，推动了中国新诗现代化的建设。“通过意象派而实现的中美诗歌艺术的借鉴与吸收，成了跨越时代、地域、语言和文化而实现异质民族文学交流对话的一个佳例。”①

同样，美国先锋（试验）戏剧从中国戏曲中寻找思想资源，同时又反过来对中国现代戏剧产生了重要影响。19 世纪末，西方具有先锋意识的剧作家认识到“幻觉剧场”的僵化性，开始向东方戏曲寻求突破的思想资源。1921 年，美国评论家威尔·欧文（Will Irwin）在《纽约时报书评周刊》上发表评论唐人街戏剧的文章，认为“中国戏剧表演是一门比我们通常在美国舞台上所见到的更为完美的艺术”②，为随后美国先锋戏剧借鉴中国戏剧艺术打开了良好的开端。美国“现代戏剧之父”尤金·奥尼尔的试验剧中采用的独白、面具、舞台分割等艺术技巧，可能来自中国戏剧的启示。其 1926 年创作的《拉撒路笑了》中，四个人物各以半个面具来表现双重人格的手法，可能是对中国京剧脸谱的运用；后期剧作中使用的插曲和循环形式，在结构模式上也与传统的中国戏曲不无相似之处。

梅兰芳 1929–1930 年在美国的巡回演出也给美国剧作家带来了革新西方写实戏剧的灵感。梅兰芳在美国演出后引起媒体和评论界的极大关注，尤其是中国戏剧舞台上的写意手法使美国戏剧界大受震动。《纽约太阳报》的评论员说：“人们不无惊奇地发现，数百年来中国演员在舞台上创造出一整套示意动作，使你感觉做得完全合情合理。”《纽约世界报》的评论员赞扬中国人“在不采用实体布景和道具方面远远超前了我们好几个世纪。我们花费成千上万的钱财使舞台上呈现实景……而

① 《中外文学交流史：中国—美国卷》，第 100 页。

② 都文伟：《百老汇的中国题材与中国戏曲》，上海三联书店 2002 年版，第 142 页。

中国人却用一些常规的示意动作代替了这些笨重的累赘”[①]。美国剧作家桑顿·怀尔德观看梅兰芳的演出后深受启发，其获普利策奖的剧作《小镇风光》上演时不设幕布和布景，仅有一张桌子、几把椅子和一个小凳子，通过移动桌椅来制造出想象中的民房、商店、马路、教堂、公墓，并设置了一个角色来介绍小镇的面貌、出场人物的性格、职业、归宿，对戏中的人和事进行评说，颇似中国传统戏曲的模式和场景。

中美戏剧的影响是双向的，不仅美国的先锋（试验）戏剧从中国传统戏曲中找到了思想资源，美国先锋戏剧也反过来对中国现代戏剧产生了影响。中国现代戏剧的奠基人之一洪深 1916 年去美国留学，时值美国先锋戏剧勃兴之时。洪深放弃实业救国的留学初衷，转而学习戏剧和导演艺术，意图通过戏剧揭示人生，改造社会。1922 年洪深回国后“将他在美国学习的现代戏剧排演及管理体制，结合中国戏剧发展的事实,进行了创造性转化”[②],极大地推动了中国现代戏剧的革新与发展，其戏剧《赵阎王》代表着中国现代戏剧从“文明戏”走向“爱美剧”的转折，“在世界文化格局里面凸现了中国文化因素”。[③]

侨易学的一个基本方法是“取象说易”。中美诗歌的“交感”在意象派诗歌中找到了“交感点”，中美戏剧的“侨化”在美国先锋戏剧和中国现代戏剧中产生了“桥交效应”，这些“交感”和“侨化”从实践层面印证、丰富着侨易学理论，显示了“精神力量的形成、观念领域的扩展和丰富”[④]。

二 异国形象塑造中的恒常

侨易学除了探讨因“侨”而致的“易”之外，还表现出对道衡的寻

---

① 梅绍武:《我的父亲梅兰芳》(上)，中华书局 2006 年版，第 226 页。
② 周宁等:《中外文学交流史：中国—美国卷》，山东教育出版社 2016 年版，第 190 页。
③ 周宁等:《中外文学交流史：中国—美国卷》，山东教育出版社 2016 年版，第 193 页。
④ 叶隽:《侨易现象的规则性问题》,《中国文学研究》2013 年第 4 期。

求，即“在变中求不变，在‘易’中求‘常’”①。在中美文学交流过程中的中美形象互塑中，带有普遍性的现象一是通常以既有的境遇为前提来想象他者，并最终指向对自身文化的认同；二是异国形象塑造中存在着大量的套话或曰定型化形象。

关于第一个现象，中美文学交流史提供了大量的例证。首先，从中国对美国的形象塑造来看，中国知识分子对美国开国总统华盛顿的推崇隐含着中国人对尧舜模式的追寻；中国文坛对美国作家辛克莱的重视是左翼文学语境下的时代选择。

鸦片战争之后的很长一段时间内，凡是有关美国的介绍文字几乎都少不了对华盛顿的推崇，这和近代中华民族危难之际人们对于国家自强的热望有密切关系。在近代中国人的想象里，华盛顿是抗击英国殖民主义的英雄，是美国的开国元勋，有着中国上古尧舜的贤明。近代中国知识分子对民主的想象使得他们渴望中国“能够出现一个华盛顿式的领导者，荡涤一切颓败局势以造就一个全新体制的国家”②，华盛顿成为当时苦苦寻求国家出路的爱国人士心目中的航标。但“值得特别注意的是，近代中国人对于华盛顿及美国形态的理解一直是以中国上古的圣贤明君和礼制王道的既有形态为蓝本而建构起来的，它实际上代表的只是‘尧舜’模式的现实想象，而绝非是对美国的那种现代国家体制及其‘自由’、‘民主’、‘平等’和‘法制’等观念的真正理解，其中包含的主要是近代士人对现实政治的不满，那种由历代知识分子共同构筑起来的‘三代礼制’的‘王道’理想从蛰伏状态被再次重新唤醒了……‘美国’在此仅仅只是‘尧舜’模式的现实替代形态而已。”③

同样，20世纪20年代末30年代初中国文坛对美国作家厄普敦·辛克莱的普遍欢迎是当时中国左翼文学思潮的产物。1930年“左联”的成立使得左翼的无产阶级文学成为时代的主流，而辛克莱作为美国本土的左翼作家，其对资本主义社会罪恶本质的揭露与批判更能体现

---

① 叶隽：《变创与渐常：侨易学的概念》，北京大学出版社2014年版，第20页。

② 周宁等：《中外文学交流史：中国—美国卷》，山东教育出版社2016年版，第17页。

③ 周宁等：《中外文学交流史：中国—美国卷》，山东教育出版社2016年版，第17页。

资本主义制度的腐朽性、没落性和无产阶级革命的必然性、正义性，能让更多的人认清形势，投身到全球性的红色革命中去。应当说辛克莱的创作恰好契合了 20 世纪 30 年代中国左翼文学的需求。因而，“对于 30 年代的中国文坛来说，辛克莱基本上已经成为了勇敢地以文学为武器向着资本主义和帝国主义开火的战斗者的最为优秀的代表”。① 言说他者的背后是对自我的言说，一国关于他国的形象实际上折射的是自我的欲望和需求，想象他者只能以自身的既有境遇为前提。

其次，美国文学中对中国形象的塑造最终是从他者这面镜子中返观和确认自身。1877 年，马克·吐温和布莱特·哈特合作的剧本《阿新》（*Ah Sin*）塑造了一个滑稽、神秘、无知、柔弱的华人男性形象，在对中国文化“低劣、幼稚、阴柔”的表述中，实现的是对“文明、发达、强大”的美国文化的认同。② 剧本中白人对阿新的“同情”、“爱抚”和“保护”，暗示出美国意欲“帮助”中国走向“文明、开化”的强烈欲望。③ 奥尼尔 1925 年创作的以中国元朝为背景的剧本《马可百万》（*Marco Millions*）塑造了两个具有强烈对比意味的人物形象——西方商人马可·波罗和中国公主阔阔真。前者追求物质利益，冷漠、僵硬，缺乏美好的人性人情；后者追求精神生活，宽厚、温情、充满活力。“剧作中被想象、美化了的‘中国’形象，是一种乌托邦化的文化他者”，④ 奥尼尔意在“通过东西方的对比，反思西方的物质主义”⑤，其目的仍是对自我文化的认同。

美国文学作品中所塑造的定型化中国形象或曰套话，也在一定程度上体现了异民族互察中的某种通律。中国形象在美国人眼中虽然如万花筒一般多变，但“中国佬”、“黄祸”等定型化形象却具有持久性和多语境性。

和“中国佬”有关的两个套话是“中国佬约翰”与“异教徒中国

---

① 《中外文学交流史：中国—美国卷》，第 12 页。
② 《中外文学交流史：中国—美国卷》，第 55 页。
③ 《中外文学交流史：中国—美国卷》，第 57 页。
④ 《中外文学交流史：中国—美国卷》，第 62 页。
⑤ 《中外文学交流史：中国—美国卷》，第 61 页。

佬”。前者在美国较早出现在1855年发表于《加利福尼亚歌者》（*The California Songster*）上的《中国佬约翰》（*John Chinaman*），诗中的“中国佬约翰”口蜜腹剑，撒谎、偷盗、欺骗样样齐全。20多年后马克·吐温和布莱特·哈特合作的剧本《阿新》中，华人阿新诡秘、怪异、不可理解，“中国佬约翰”的套话再次释放出能量，甚至为美国词汇增添了一句生动的短语：“像中国佬那样毫无机会。”后者“异教徒中国佬”源于布莱特·哈特1870年写的一首幽默讽刺诗《诚实的詹姆斯的老实话》（*Plain Language from Truthful James*），诗中的华人阿新以各种阴险古怪的方式，耍弄愚蠢的把戏，逗得美国公众捧腹大笑，后来该诗以《异教徒中国佬》（*The Heathen Chinee*）之名在美国家喻户晓。“异教徒”本是基督徒对非基督徒的称谓，但和“中国佬”连在一起便“包含了落后、卑贱、愚昧、狡诈、恶毒、阴险、自私、残暴、肮脏、顽固，以及天真、沉默、神秘、忍耐等等的低层次的人性蕴涵”，成为美国人辨识中国人形象的一个标识，“甚至到了第二次世界大战时期，美国总统罗斯福还习惯性地以此称呼中国人，‘每当他描述他不喜欢的人时，他就使用这样的字眼——中国佬’。”[①]套话“中国佬”的顽固性由此可见一斑。

“黄祸”套话起源于1895年德国皇帝威廉二世的说法，他曾命宫廷画家赫尔曼·奈克法斯画了一幅名为《黄祸》的版画，使得“黄祸”一词很快在欧洲流传开来。描写黄祸的美国作家有惠特尼（Atwell Whitney）、沃尔特（Robert Wolter）、杜纳（Pierton W. Dooner）、钱伯斯（Robert W. C hambers）、诺尔（William Norr）等人，而将“黄祸”想象推向极端并最终创造出影响至深的“黄祸”化身“傅满洲”形象的是萨克斯·罗默（Sax Rohmer）。在罗默的“傅满洲”系列小说中，中国人多以黑社会暴徒、战争狂人、异教魔鬼、危险的入侵者等面目出现，美国人在想象中制造出一个邪恶的假想敌，实际上是对东方民族心生恐惧的极端表现。而且这种发自心底的恐惧在持续不断的强化之后，沉淀为美国人的集体无意识，在适合的时机会沉渣泛起。冷战时期，

① 《中外文学交流史：中国—美国卷》，第44页。

"黄祸"变成"红祸"和"红色威胁"，主宰了美国官方对中国的认识。在民族与民族的互察中，关于异族的套话几乎是一种普遍的存在，这种现象可视为侨易学中对道衡的追求，是对侨易规律的一种把握。

三 侨易个体位移中的观念创生

在侨易学阐释中，选择个案入手是比较容易把握的，而且在侨易学观念中，因物质位移或精神漫游而造成的个体思想观念形成与创生的例子比比皆是。我们以胡适的物质位移所带来的文学观念创建、爱默生与梭罗对儒家思想的精神漫游而创生的超验主义哲学的侨动过程，来"观侨释理"，考察其中流力区的形成。

胡适在留学美国期间受到包括意象派在内的多种现代诗派的吸引，特别是在意象派诗歌的影响下，提出了他的具有开创意义的"八不主义"，即中国的文学革新必需努力做到以下八点：须言之有物、不模仿古人、须讲求文法、不作无病之呻吟、务去滥调套词、不用典、不讲对仗、不避俗字俗语。如若将这八点和庞德发表于 1913 年的《一个意象主义者的几个不作》中对于诗歌语言的八项规定相比，其渊源关系可以看得十分清楚。当然，胡适不是在机械地借鉴意象派的信条，而是根据中国文学的现状对之进行改造，并"由此开辟了中国文学的全新格局"[①]。而他所翻译的美国女诗人萨拉·蒂斯黛尔（Sara Teasdale）的《在屋顶上》(*Over the Roof*)（胡适译为《关不住了》）则构成了他的"新诗成立的纪元"[②]。胡适 1920 年出版的《尝试集》是我国第一部新诗集，同年他提出的"诗体大解放""掀起中国新诗运动的先声"，"对于创立和发展中国新诗具有重大意义"。[③]

较之胡适的物质位移带来的文学观念的更新，爱默生、梭罗则通过

---

① 周宁等:《中外文学交流史：中国—美国卷》，山东教育出版社 2016 年版，第 97 页。

② 胡适:《尝试集·再版自序》，人民文学出版社 1987 年版，第 186 页。

③ 周宁等:《中外文学交流史：中国—美国卷》，山东教育出版社 2016 年版，第 71 页。

对儒家思想的精神漫游，创立了他们的超验主义哲学。中国学界倾向于认为爱默生、梭罗在欧洲文化的基础上，接受了儒家、佛教、伊斯兰教等东方古典思想的影响，形成他们的超验论。爱默生和梭罗曾在不同时期表达过对中国古代圣哲的敬意，他们的著述中也多次出现儒家思想的语录式言论。应当说，“以孔孟为代表的儒家思想确实对爱默生及梭罗的‘超验论’思想产生过积极的影响”。[①] 首先，超验主义追求宇宙统一的思想，与儒家强调人的内在精神和外在自然相统一的认识极为契合，令反思西方理性主义过度膨胀之后造成人与自然相分离、对抗的爱默生与梭罗，产生强烈的共鸣。其次，儒家强调个人修为的做法对超验主义者追求“人格精神的自立及对纯粹物质主义的排斥”也有深刻的启发，他们从儒家的“修身”和“性善”论中“体悟到了某种对抗加尔文教的所谓‘人性堕落’及对‘上帝’的无条件依从等等教诲的新力量”。[②] 最后，儒家“吾日三省吾身”的内省与超验主义的“直观”“领悟”也有相当程度的吻合。诚然，爱默生和梭罗对于东方思想并非全盘吸收，而是取其契合之点为我所用。儒家思想仅是超验主义的源头之一，而且这一源头在“异质性的环境”中发生了“精神质变”，最终形成对美国文学影响深远的超验论思想。

异质性、关联性、整体性，相互关系、交互作用、万物交感，观念更新、思想质变、规律把握，碰撞、迁变、创生……这些关键词既是中外文学交流所关注与践行的，也是侨易学观念所致力追求的。侨易学新颖的哲思方式为跨文化的中美文学交流提供了方法论的指导，中美文学交流亦为侨易学理论提供了坚实的实证大地。

参考文献：

都文伟：《百老汇的中国题材与中国戏曲》，上海三联书店 2002 年版。

胡适：《尝试集・再版自序》，人民文学出版社 1987 年版。

梅绍武：《我的父亲梅兰芳》（上），中华书局 2006 年版。

① 《中外文学交流史：中国—美国卷》，第 92 页。

② 《中外文学交流史：中国—美国卷》，第 92 页。

叶隽:《变创与渐常：侨易学的概念》，北京大学出版社 2014 年版。
叶隽:《侨易现象的规则性问题》,《中国文学研究》2013 年第 4 期。
叶隽:《侨易学的观念》,《教育学报》2011 年第 2 期。
赵毅衡:《意象派与中国古典诗歌》,《外国文学研究》1979 年第 4 期。
周宁、朱徽、贺昌盛、周云龙:《中外文学交流史：中国—美国卷》，山东教育出版社 2016 年版。

文学的“侨寓”与“翻易”：以中美戏剧文学交流为例

周云龙 *

Abstract The literature relation between nations brings out the dynamic of development. Diaspora and exile literature that have the symbolic meaning lay the foundation for the study of transnational literature relations. The exchange dynamic of Sino-America theatre literature origins from the difference between the traditions of their performance cultures. The history of Sino-America theatre literature exchange tells how the two performance cultures see each other as cultural other and exceed themselves. It is necessary to highlight the premise of the history writing because this premise decides the topic that Chinese and American theatres' tactics to remap and engage the world literature picture.

Keywords diaspora; translation; literature relation between China and the foreign

---

* 作者为福建师范大学文学院教授，博士生导师，主要从事比较文学形象学和跨文化戏剧研究。

一

1935年年初，鲁迅在为其责编的《〈中国新文学大系〉小说二集》作“序言”时写道：“蹇先艾叙述过贵州，裴文中关心着榆关，凡在北京用笔写出他的胸臆来的人们，无论他自称为用主观或客观，其实往往是乡土文学，从北京这方面说，则是侨寓文学的作者。但这又非如勃兰兑斯（G. Brandes）所说的‘侨民文学’，侨寓的只是作者自己，却不是这作者所写的文章，因此也只见隐现着乡愁，很难有异域情调来开拓读者的心胸，或者炫耀他的眼界。……”这句话提出的“侨寓”概念，意即某人离开故乡、寓居他乡。在勃兰兑斯的“侨民文学”（今译“流亡文学”）的参照框架中，鲁迅委婉地表达了他对“五四”一代青年作家的遗憾与期待——摒弃自身的侨寓，实践文学的侨寓。勃兰兑斯在其《十九世纪文学主流》第一分册中，讨论了18、19世纪之交法国知识界的“流亡”现象：在一部分彼此际遇迥异的法国知识分子身上，同时体现出一种反抗的气质——接受18世纪的“帝国”遗产，但拒不承担义务，在新世纪里发展新设想。这些流亡在外的法国知识分子，“对整个法国传播了有关别国特点和文化的知识。”无疑，鲁迅的人生经验和文化实践对这个年代的这批法国知识分子更容易发生精神间的共鸣，所以，鲁迅心目中的“新文学”应该就是勃兰兑斯“侨民文学”/“流亡文学”的中国版本。

鲁迅20世纪30年代的文学理想与文化愿景，在当代后结构主义哲学家（比如，我们耳熟能详的罗兰·巴特、福柯、德里达、拉康、德勒兹等人）构建的知识脉络中，不仅更易于理解，而且可以推得（比鲁迅的“启蒙”旨归）更远。真正的“侨寓文学”，应该祛除文学创作主体的“人格化”倾向，相反，真正的主体是无名的，而是呈现为一种所谓的立体、流动的“关系体系”。从比较文学学科史的角度，如果说18、19世纪之交法国知识界的“流亡”构成了稍后的学科萌芽与自觉——我们不应该忘记作为这支“流亡”队伍中的一员的斯塔尔夫人，日后对比较文学学科形成的巨大贡献，那么，鲁迅的“遗憾与期待”（或《〈中国新文学大系〉小说二集》“序言”本身）同样可以视为现代中国比较文学学科诞生的“宣言”之一。

无论是鲁迅期望的“侨寓文学”，还是勃兰兑斯命名的“流亡文学”，在根本上，其努力方向就是“传播有关别国特点和文化的知识”，二者均体现为一种文学创作的跨国族、跨文化互动视野。换句话说，它们都需要在“关系”之间运作；反之亦然，国族间的文化、文学“关系”构成了二者自我成就的内在机制和知识动力。虽然在域外作品译介和学术研究中，早已出现了国族间的文化、文学“关系”的互动实践，但从理论（的自觉）构建上说，“侨寓文学”和“流亡文学”这两个具有象征意义的文学术语或“比较”观念，一定程度上分别在中国和欧洲，为后来的跨国文学关系研究奠定了理论基础。

二

经过百年的垦拓、传承与积累，如今，“中外文学交流史”已是中国比较文学研究领域中相对较为成熟的板块。“交流”本身就是一种关系形式的描述，因此用于清理和评判文学间的事实联系的“影响研究”依然是该研究的基本范式。但是，兴起于现代“民族主义”历史—社会背景下的影响研究，暗含着“我施你受”的权力关系，它假设在一种二元对立的两极关系中——其中的一极永远处于被动、沉默的状态，这是我们在运用该范式进行研究时必须予以反思和超越的。在此，我们以中国和美国的文学交流历史为例，就可以看出，作为一个年轻的移民国家，美国极力地需要确认其民族文化身份。20 世纪 20 年代，以格拉斯培尔、奥尼尔等为代表的剧作家们开始反思欧洲戏剧传统，努力摆脱欧洲戏剧、特别是英国戏剧的影响，致力创作以反映美国历史与现实、表现美国人民思想情绪和审美理想、融合美国民间艺术成分的戏剧样式。就这个层面而言，中美两国的戏剧艺术在 20 世纪初面临着相似的文化境遇。但是，美国和西欧属于同质文化圈，曾经是英属北美殖民地的美国也继承了西欧文化中的扩张心态。这就决定了在某种特定的历史情势下，在异质的中美戏剧文化遭遇的空间中，也不可避免地存在着一种支配关系。检视中美戏剧交流的历史，亦可发现这种几乎贯穿始终的不对称的交流状况，而中国戏剧文化始终处于弱势。这样一来，我们在描述中美戏剧文学交流历史的时候，就要对中美戏剧交流的描述立场保持审慎的态度，反思既往影响研究的局限性。

正如勃兰兑斯和鲁迅提出的“流亡文学”和“侨寓文学”各自所处的特定的法国和中国历史语境，中国和美国的戏剧文学交流的动力亦来自于两种戏剧文化传统间的差异，因此，中美戏剧交流的历史，同时也是彼此互为文化他者，确认、否定并超越自我的历史。提出这一历史描述的立场和研究、写作的前提是必要的。这一写作立场决定了“中美戏剧文学交流史”的主旨是要探讨时间向度上的贯穿性问题，即在中美戏剧间的双向互动的各个历史阶段，二者是如何借助对方完成各自的“世界性”参与和“现代性”转化的。

在“传播有关别国特点和文化的知识”时，遭遇的第一问题就是文学译介中的语言问题。20 世纪 80 年代以来，翻译研究领域发生文化转向，侧重点由既往的是否忠实原作转移到翻译中的文化权力以及在目标语境中的文化功能。这个转向潜在地对既有的国别文学交流史研究和写作带来很多冲击。廖炳惠、朱耀伟等学者都曾借用罗伯特 · J. C. 扬的观点，主张把 translation 译 /“易”为“翻易”，就是在强调跨文化译介过程中的翻译，同时也是改易的过程，它更强调“分歧、断裂、演现效果”。文化批评领域的这一实践成果，对我们审视、重构“影响—接受”的文化交流模式有着诸多启迪。

在“影响—接受”的文化交流模式中，处于弱势的一极并非完全处于被动状态，它面对强势文化的覆盖性冲击，往往会主动地加以判断、选择和创造；同时，它亦会给予强势文化造成回馈性影响，虽然二者存在着明显的话语逆差。这种事实存在于中美戏剧交流的整个历史进程中，该研究正是从这个思考基点和基本观念出发，清理中美戏剧交流的事实，并分析这个交流历史所隐喻的两种文化主体的自身认同。比如，自 20 世纪 20 年代后期开始，奥尼尔在中国的译介密度越来越大，其影响的发生几乎和中国现代戏剧（包括戏曲）的现代转型的历史同步。从洪深、曹禺到李龙云的戏剧观念和创作，还有借用其戏剧题材的戏曲创作，都能够看到奥尼尔的戏剧思想的影响。但是，奥尼尔对于中国现代戏剧的影响的结果，并非中美文化“杂交”后的戏剧“混血儿”，更多的是一种“启示”——为中国现代戏剧的进一步发展贡献了一块可供熔铸的基石；而中国戏剧家们在判断、选择基础上的创造性成果，反过来也为“世界”现代戏剧艺术谱系增添无可替代的东方戏剧艺术精神。中国传统戏曲艺术随着 19 世纪末赴美华工一起登陆美国，作为一种社区文化活动，不仅具有缓解乡愁和族群认同的社会动员功能，还为美国借鉴戏曲手法的实验戏剧的形成，提供了部分重要的灵感。梅兰芳在 1930 年访美演出，更是中国戏剧的世界参与和现代转型的一次自觉实践。这次演出，从世界性的文化视野中反证了本土戏曲艺术的价值，成为中国戏曲现代转型的一个重要契机，同时也给美国的先锋艺术家带来了一定的影响。同样，美国的艺术家亦从中进行了判断和选择，并进行了价值置换，他们真正认同的是西方的古老戏剧传统。在观众的参与、选择、共享与创造中，美国剧作家征用中国题材与异国情调，致力于“中国性”的表述。美国戏剧的“中国”想象经历了一个从“阿新”到“阔阔真”，再到“蝴蝶君”这样一个多面、驳杂的过程。从总体上看，“中国”一直徘徊在低劣和美好的两极之间。虽然西方戏剧中的“中国”都在不同的尺度上强调其“真实”，但它们与现实的中国没有直接的必然联系，是“美国臆想之中国”。在中美戏剧文化双向交流的历史中，两种戏剧文化无一例外地都履行了各自的文化主体的自身认同功能，双方都扮演了一个文化他者的角色。

上述具有反思性的“影响—接受”的文化交流模式，或者说是一种双向的“影响——反哺”模式，在理论背景上，具有明显的后殖民主义文化批判的“反写”色彩。这种文学“翻易”研究尝试着反思并超越既往的文学关系研究所一贯采纳的影响研究范式的局限性，同时兼顾“影响的积极意义”和“影响的负面意义”：既注意发掘双方如何通过互动、交流完成各自的“世界性”参与和“现代性”转化，同时解构影响中的文化“霸权”因素，凸显出作为弱势的一极的中国戏剧文学的主体性。但是，既然文学交流呈现为一种互为他者的关系，那么，我们也可以说，美国戏剧在想象中国的时候，中国戏剧也在想象、运用着对方。因此，我们在揭示了美国戏剧的中国想象后，还必须讨论中国戏剧如何同时也利用了这一机制想象自身和美国戏剧的事实，以及这种双向想象和运用之间的逻辑关联问题。这是对于中美戏剧交流历史的研究终结处一个必然会出现的问题。

如果说影响研究范式中存在着显而易见的二元对立的两极模式，那么，上述试图反思和超越这种二元模式的同时，恰恰又反向地运用了“影响式”结构与思维定式。就在笔者致力于解构影响中国的美国戏剧文化中的霸权因素时，又建构了新的二元对立模式。这种呈现“中国戏剧”主体性的两难困境，迫使自己追问：“中国”的意义是否只能在反抗西方强势话语中得以发生？于是，开启别样的资源与视野，成为文学关系史研究面临的迫切问题。

三

中外文学交流史研究是否既可以解构全球主义历史进程所构建的西方中心的世界秩序，还可以淡化后殖民主义文化批判框架中所暗隐的敌意和对立，在国别文学、文化间达成一种有益的对话与协商？在这样的思考与追问中，我们不妨引入另一个诠释脉络，即尝试以侨易观念——这一基本的哲学工具，切入文学交流史的写作。

侨易观念体现为一种整体性思维，它试图提供追寻文明、宇宙大道的思想资源。通过对侨学、《易经》哲学思想的现代阐释，在方法论的层面，侨易观念强调在考察思想变迁的过程中，要“观侨取象，察变寻异”。这个动态的过程又暗隐着两个层次：在“二元三维”的分析框架中思考思想观念在漫长的变迁、侨动、变易过程中讨论异质文化碰撞、互动关系中的“交易”，其重心在于“变创”；还有一个重要的意义向度，就是这个过程中的“不易”或“渐常”。在“易变”或“变创”的层次中，侨动的思想观念将不属于二元格局中的任何一极，因为它们的意义始终都在互动流转，不存在一个孤立恒定、本质主义的文化特质，这将对异质文化交流中的不均衡格局构成有力的挑战。但侨易的理论动能并未到此为止。从“不易”或“渐常”的角度着眼，侨易观念最富于创造力的理论层面就是，其关注点从二元格局中，找到了具有超越单极视野的“第三维”。这个“第三维”的浮现，需要把理论视点投注于既有二元文化格局之“间”的“流力因素”上。这一步“具有重要意义，因为如此就构成了三维结构，是个稳定性结构。……但这个三元结构不是实体三元，因为那个‘三’可能永远不是完整意义上可以与‘二’抗衡之‘三’。”这等于宣示了侨易观念的“第三维”其实是一种立场和方法，它并不与“二元”处于同一范畴，它拒绝既有的二元抗衡游戏，从而使自身具有了哲学的意义。因为在二元的“游戏场”中的任何一极都必定是觊觎场中的各种资本、并且试图调整自身文化位置的棋子，当它试图获取资本的同时，就“总是已经”（always-already）默认并受制于场中的游戏规则。“第三维”不再假设对抗与对立，不再把资本与权力视为一种绝对的中心，而是以一种文化间沟通、转换、契合之后的见道之思将其包容。侨易观念的“第三维”所孜孜寻求的文化间沟通与转化的契合点，彼此间的相似性，或者说是思想观念侨动中的“不易”或“渐常”。因此，侨易观念内在地具有一种跨文化对话的伦理关怀与诉求。

借助侨易观念提供的分析框架，文学交流史写作也许可以采取一种本土的批判反思立场，同时关注西方文学在中国现代语境中再生产知识、权力的关系的中间媒介，即中西二元之下的第三个维度。在这样的基本观念和思路中，仍以中美戏剧文学交流史为例，我们可以试图发掘西方戏剧“知识”如何借助留美归国的现代知识分子的跨文化实践，“旅行”到中国本土，并在这一繁复的语境中被现代中国知识分子想象和运用，生发新的意义的内在机制。比如张彭春、洪深、余上沅、熊佛西等人的跨文化戏剧实践，在特定的中国语境中的文化位置的微妙转化中，便蕴含着这样的议题。从这种本土的批判立场出发，可以有效地超越某种简单的主体立场。我们在关注西方影响中的“霸权”因素时，借助的往往是西方的理论资源，比如西方现代知识分子用于反思自身的问题的后殖民主义文化批判等。这些理论固然可以解构西方中心主义话语，但同时又遮蔽了西方文化的自我批判反思意识，我们移植了西方的问题，却丢掉了西方的精神。如果我们借助侨易观念中的"二元思维"框架中蕴含的自我批判精神用于自身的反思，则可以彻底撼动文化霸权的哲学前提，即二元对立的思维模式，在研究中凸显一种间性伦理和对话精神。

再回到勃兰兑斯和鲁迅的"流亡文学"和"侨寓文学"，我们可以说，从彼此如何借助对方完成各自的"世界性"参与和"现代性"转化这样一个基本问题出发，勾勒历史的线条并索解其文化含义，当时跨国文学交流历史研究的源点性议题。跨国文学交流历史研究既是一个相对独立自足的学术领域，更是一个流动、开放的思想场域，它也经历了从追寻主体性、解构强势文化霸权到试图超越主体立场，这么一个不断自我反思，吸纳其他观念方法，实现自我超越的过程。因此，在内在的观念与方法上，该领域始终保留着不断走向成熟的痕迹，它的每一次"出发"都将会开启无限的可能。

参考文献：

鲁迅：《且介亭杂文二集 ·〈中国新文学大系〉小说二集序》，《鲁迅全集》，第 6 卷，人民文学出版社 1981 年版。

[丹麦] 勃兰兑斯：《十九世纪文学主流 · 第一分册：流亡文学》，张道真译，人民文学出版社 2009 年版，第 1–3 页。

朱耀伟：《香港（研究）作为方法：关于"香港论述"的可能性》，周云龙主编《圆桌》2015 春夏卷，总第 1 期，人民出版社 2015 年版，第 98 页。

叶隽：《变创与渐常：侨易学的观念》，北京大学出版社 2014 年版，第 14–15 页。

中外文学交流中的生态和侨易“身份”

张　华*

Abstract　This paper examines the identity of literature in Chinese and American, Chinese and Canadian volumes of *History of Chinese and Foreign Literature Exchange*, and explains the concept, object and framework of Qiao-Yiology. It puts forward a new understanding of the concept of ecology in the study of the history of Sino-foreign literary exchanges or relations, and how to grasp the law of the transformation of Sino-foreign literary relations from the perspective of Qiao-Yiology.

Keywords　literary relation; ecology; Qiao-Yiology; identity

一

美国著名生态批评学者帕特里克·墨菲（Patrick D. Murphy）教授曾说：人类作为自然世界的一部分，与整个自然的其他方面始终存在一

*　作者为北京语言大学比较文学与世界文学专业教授，博士生导师，《中美比较文学》集刊中方主编。

种“动态均衡”的进程，这是一种没有专属于人类特权条件的“动态均衡”，是由生物圈中每一个存在体参与和互动的“动态平衡”。人与其他生物从未保持过一种不变的“姿态”，而是在不断地从一种不平衡状态走向另一个方向的不平衡。每一次变化、维持和复位，都有难以预测的反响和结果，这些反响和结果都需要我们通过文化和经济活动的改变来进行处理和矫正。作为进化的产物，我们并非一个终结的存在，不像一个完成的商品，被放在货架之上等待售出、等待消费。我们应该把自己更多地理解为一个更大的多元生物进程环链中的进程之一，而相对于更小的生物进程，我们又是其更大的多元生物进程环链。我们生活在一个生态系统中的同时，细菌、寄生虫和病毒生活在我们体内，也还生活在他们自己的生态系统中。[①] 如果我们用这样一种观念来审视文学、文学史，特别是文学交流史，它们将都是“流动的”、“行旅式的”或“处在进程中的”。

毫无疑问，一部文学作品，从作家开始创作直到最终“完成”，始终处于一种动态进程当中；即使在“完成”之后，阅读、接受、批评和诠释等“再创造”当然也是处于动态的进程当中。就此意义上来讲，文学史的写作和叙述，是叙述者对作者和读者之动态进程的“总结”，显然，这种所谓的“总结”也是处于一种动态的进程之中的。中外文学交流史，自不必多论，“中外”“文学”“交流”和“史”，每一个概念之谓均是“流动状态”的体现，即“生动的状态”，也就是帕特里克·墨菲所理解的“生态”。可以说，由钱林森、周宁教授主编、山东教育出版社出版的多卷本《中外文学交流史》就从各个方面体现了中外文学交流史的这样一种“生态”。正如加拿大学者亚历山大·比科洛福特（Alexander Beecroft）博士在其新著《世界文学的一种生态：从古代到今天》中所说，既有的文学与它形成过程中的文化、政治、经济即“环境”之间构成了复杂的互动关系，在这样的互动关系中穿过时空来考察

---

① 帕特里克·墨菲著，张华译：《作为自然之部分的人》，载《鄱阳湖学刊》2016 年第 3 期。

文学流变的过去和今天，就构成了文学产生和交流的“生态”。[①]

《中外文学交流史》总序中说，中外文学交流史的叙事方式当属中外文学关系研究，而这种研究仍然属于传统范型，面临着新问题新观念的挑战。然而，在我看来，这部看似传统研究方式的文学交流史，却从不同层面支持了当今比较文学研究领域许多新理论、新方法和新体系（比如，侨易学）的建构和实践。以本文的篇幅，难以对《中外文学交流史》皇皇十七卷均作侨易学透视，即使对中加、中美这两卷恢宏之作的每一个部分做整体的详尽评述，也难以实现。所以，只能以一斑窥全豹，撷取其中“侨”与“易”得以最明显、最充分体现的华裔文学部分，特别是针对“文化身份”问题，通过侨易学视角和方法进行辨析，亦为读后之感，供方家批评。

二

尽管德国思想家雅思贝尔斯（Karl T. Jaspers）回避了对“轴心时代”物质位移的研究，提出虽然中国、印度、中东和希腊之间有千山万水的阻隔，但它们在轴心时代的文化却有很多相通的地方。然而，人类考古和历史地理学可以证明，人类的迁徙从古至今从来没有停止过，兴许古今迁徙的原因各有不同，但从频率和规模上相对来看，古代人的迁徙并不比我们今天微弱。古代的旅行虽不像今天的旅行，但从物质位移到精神易变的过程必有相似之处。哥白尼日心说带来的思想革命甚至胜过今天每一次大的思想革命，踏足北美新大陆的第一步与人类登上月球的“一小步”具有同样的“一大步”意义。也正是在新大陆发现之后，作家、思想家越来越看重物质位移与精神易变的动态关联，比如在法国，蒙田（Montaigne）的《文集》（*Essays*）和孟德斯鸠（Montesquieu）的《波斯人信札》（*Persian letters*）就是如此。

---

① Alexander Beecroft (2015), *An Ecology of World Literature: From Antiquity to the Present Day*, Verso, p.157.

侨易学，作为一种新颖的哲思方式与方法论，其基本理念是因“侨”而致“易”，前者强调空间维度的整合，后者关注时间维度的演进，其中既包括物质位移、精神漫游所造成的个体思想观念形成与创生，也包括不同的文化子系统如何相互作用与精神变形。应用于文学交流史研究，侨易视域注重观侨取象、取象察变、察变求易，由此寻找文学交流史中“大道不变，细流涌动”之规律性结论，[①] 因为“无论何种具体内容，其实都摆不脱基本的流转变易的整体框架，这正是侨易思维的特长所在。”[②] 以侨易视域来审视中美、中加文学交流史和或关系史可以考察双方文学作品本身体现的形象性或意象性侨易，即文学作品所记录、描述或虚构的形象的行游或行旅，这类作品在《中外文学交流史》中美、中加卷中有大量呈现；也可以考察作者本人的地理性侨易经验和精神变迁等侨易特征，同时，还可以进行跨文化侨易的文学交流与互动性思考。对于后两者，《中外文学交流史》中美卷提供了一个当代中国学术界逐渐熟悉代表人物，即美国作家梭罗（H .D. Thoreau）。

梭罗为中国学术界所熟识，源于中国对生态文学、生态批评和生态美学的研究，然而，如果我们换一个视域来察看梭罗本人和他的作品，则会有新的发现。他熟谙超验主义哲学，他创造了一种游动观念和思想，其中包括实践人的意识和人可沉思自然。他反对工业革命对工人阶级带来的疏离，他逃离尘嚣移至瓦尔登湖附近的写作正是哲学“漫游”的体现，也是对所谓社会和政治规则的自由性反叛。他说，生命存在于荒野中，极致的荒野是最鲜活的生命。[③] 随后，哲学意义上的“我思”不再是自主性的，而成为行旅性的“我思”，挑战了笛卡尔的“我思故我在”。实际上，梭罗认为，人是在动态中的人、是在“生态”中的人，人与有着同样意识的森林、河流、山川、树木、动物等共同作用，改变着陆地、海洋和天空。在现象学意义上，他的自由意识和独立思想之与权力、社会以及基本价值的关系，紧紧与其“漫游”的观念相关联。在

---

① 叶隽：《变创与渐常：侨易学的观念》，北京大学出版社 2014 年版，第 32–39 页。

② 叶隽主编，《侨易》（第一辑），社会科学文献出版社 2014 年版，第 2 页。

③ Thoreau, H. D. *Walking in Walden, Civil Disobedience, and Other Writings* (Norton Critical Editions), New-York, W. W. Norton & Company, 2008, p.274.

同样的意义上，所以有人把尼采的《查拉图斯特拉如是说》也视作哲学意义上的“漫游”，因为他对“查拉图斯特拉”的写作明显与其从拉帕罗到尼斯的“位移”有关。[①]

梭罗的侨易学价值还不仅仅停留于此。《中外文学交流史》中美卷第三章第一节“爱默生、梭罗及其对儒家思想的接受”中说：“深受爱默生‘超验论’思想影响的另一位诗人哲学家就是梭罗，梭罗很早就是爱默生所组织的‘超验主义俱乐部’的重要成员之一，这位年仅45岁就过早辞世的思想家以其更为激进的姿态将超验主义发挥到了极致。”“梭罗的思想在其既有的欧洲文化基础上，都曾不同程度地接受过东方古典思想的影响，其中包括了佛教、伊斯兰教及以孔孟为代表的中国儒家思想的诸多元素，无论是在他们的著述中，还是在他们所创办的《日晷》杂志的“各族圣经”栏目里，都随处可见东方哲人的身影。爱默生与梭罗对于中国古典哲学思想的接受主要来自于早期流传到欧洲和美国的《论语》、《孟子》及《四书》等著作，儒家思想的语录式言论也多次出现在他们各自的著述中，他们自己也在不同的时期表达过对于中国古代圣哲的由衷的敬意。”[②] 显然，梭罗作为作者的地理性侨易经验和精神变迁等侨易特征包括其思想观念的形成、在俱乐部同其他名人的交往、虽未到过中国却从东方作品中汲取思想灵感等。然而，这也只是侨易学所追求的一个层面的意涵。在此基础之上，侨易学视域还通过对经典文本以及作家的研究，进行中外文学交流多元文化互动过程及其范式的规律性探索。从理论层面来看，则是从侨易现象到侨易空间的建构，从多向度多层面的流动性，考察恒常性和元一性。另外，如上所述，梭罗在今天引起中国学者的研究兴趣，其实也恰好是一种“回侨”现象，也很值得探析。

---

① Ecce Homo, “Zarathustra”, 1–4 in Nietzsche, *The Anti-Christ, Ecce Homo, Twilight of the Idols: And Other Writings*, Cambridge, Cambridge University Press, 2005.

② 钱林森、周宁主编：《中外文学交流史：中国—美国卷》（中美卷），山东教育出版社2016年版，第91–92页。

三

身份，常常是中外文学交流中最为引人注目的关键词，《中外文学交流史》中美、中加卷全文各个章节都潜在地关注和贯穿着这样一个关键词，华裔文学部分更是明确围绕这一关键词进行了叙事和书写。中外文学交流史，顾名思义就是中外文学关系史，就是中外文学关系的流变史，运用侨易视域不仅可以研究中外文学关系的个体或群体的流变或互动关系，更可将在美国和加拿大的华裔文学作为侨易典型来进行阐释，在此层面上，身份这一关键词，可以成为凝聚和体现“侨”和“易”观念的集中“抓手”。

《中外文学交流史：中国—美国卷》第七章第一节“华裔族群的身份诉求”中有这样两段描述：

> 如果说此前的美华作家主要是在叙写华裔族群在美国生存与奋斗的真实历史的话，那么，新一代作家则以质疑与想象的方式彻底地颠覆了这段历史的真实性与合法性，由此才使隐藏于背后的构建其所谓真实历史的权力话语得以全面地暴露了出来。
>
> 新一代作家并非是要全盘否定此前作家们的创作，他们对前辈作家其实保持了足够的尊敬……新一代美华作家所面对的文化境遇也许是最为复杂和微妙的，从总体上看，他们其实一直处于至少四种势力相互碰撞的夹缝之中，在白种美国人看来，他们是“华裔”；在“唐人街”原驻华裔看来，他们是“美国人”；在美国批评家眼里，他们书写的是“中国故事”因而不属于“美国文学”；而在华裔批评家的心目中，他们又是已经被美国彻底“殖民化”了的“美国作家”，他们的所谓“中国书写”已经完全失去了“中国”特性，不过是“文化殖民”的另一种翻版，所以理应被排除在“华裔作家”之外。由于有了来自各个方向的多重力量的挤压，他们的创作才不得不首先面对一个需要优先回答的迫切问题：“我”到底

是谁？……到底是谁塑造并规定了现在的“我”？“我”有没有历史？什么样的“历史”才是真实的“我”的“历史”？“我”有没有可能重新获得“我”的“历史”？……诸如此类。由此我们才会看到，出现在新一代作家笔下的各式文本，尽管都具有多重阐释的可能，但在“文化身份”的确认问题上其实始终显示着惊人的一致。①

《中外文学交流史：中国—加拿大卷》第四章第九节“百川汇海：华文作家在加拿大”中写道：

加拿大的华文文学，其实是处于两个文化系统的交叉地带：这个地带既纳入加拿大文学的范围内，也同时纳入原籍国中国文学延伸范围内。因此，它具有双重性。这个特殊位置，提供了一个弹性的中间角度。作家主体可以在这个空间驰骋想象，可以指点江山，以超越的姿态表达自己。华文文学在原籍国的接受程度无疑远远大于移居国。如何强化它的交流能量，是个挑战！如何利用交叉地带的位置发声，同样是个挑战！②

“诉求”和“挑战”均集中表明，文化身份的非本土化“变形”或“变异”不仅仅是地理意义上的，它还会影响我们的道德伦理以及思想意识形态的整体框架，并改变我们思考文化多元性和差异性的方式。针对这种身份的诉求，侨易学的研究也许可以提供一种美学视域的“解决方案”，并需要华裔文学作家的自觉。曾长时间旅居中国的法国诗人、作家维克多·谢阁兰（Victor Segalen）曾说：异国生活亦有其难得的情调，而这种异国情调的最大作用是使作家拥有想象的能力和被想象的空

① 钱林森、周宁主编，《中外文学交流史：中国—美国卷》，山东教育出版社 2016 年版，第 354–355 页。

② 钱林森、周宁主编，《中外文学交流史：中国—加拿大卷》，山东教育出版社 2016 年版，第 206 页。

间。[①]谢阁兰认为，审美多样性的快感来自自己与“他者”的不同。他曾通过观察生活在大洋洲的毛利人写成小说作品《远古人》，[②]也曾用同样的方式生活在中国的文化与文明之中，审视中国的历史、诗歌和哲学，写成了很多的作品。在这两个“位移”过程中，谢阁兰做了“身份”的反转性“侨易”，才使得他获得了对“他者”文明的审美快感：《远古人》是以塔希提岛上毛利人的“声音”在叙述，以毛利人的文化为根基，其叙事展示的是毛利人的原始神话，代表着毛利人与其环境的互动关系；而关于中国的文学作品，则又以中国的“文化身份”在叙事。总之，在我们以侨易学的视域审视文学交流、文学关系中的共同性和规律性时，就不可避免地要研究物质位移过程中所带来的精神漫游问题，比如自我身份、自我意识和自我消解等等问题。与此同时，侨易学在研究“侨”如何致“易”的基础之上，还要研究“侨”在多大程度上致“易”，以及其中复杂多元的“变与不变”之关系。

最后，在侨易学的探讨过程中，有人提出“有侨必易”（不必再研究）的看法，但我们可以看到的事实是，人们虽然每天甚至每时每刻都有物质意义上或物理意义上的位移，处于动态之中，但思想和精神上却是沉闷和死寂的。他们正需要被一定的力量去唤醒、去搅动。正如帕特里克·墨菲所言：“我始终相信，人们时常需要被各种方式所唤醒，因为人们并不了解所谓刺激元素、唤醒记忆、审美意象或效能可以在知觉中产生引爆点。很多人从不为科学研究所改变，甚至从不阅读充满数据、图形和图表的科学报告。然而，这些人很可能去读小说，去抄诗，去听歌，或去看电影，这些活动能够激起他们的情感共鸣和反响，可以在自己和共生的非人类物种之间建立起一种联结，而这些非人类物种与我们共享同一个环境，并且同生共死。”[③]在《中外文学交流史》中加卷

① Segalen, V., *Essay on Exoticism: An Aesthetics of Diversity*, translated by Yael Rachel Schlick, Durham, Duke University Press Books, 2002.

② Segalen, V. (Max Anély), *Les Immémoriaux* [1907], Paris, Terre humaine Poche, Paris, 2009.

③ 帕特里克·墨菲著、张华译：《作为自然之部分的人》，载《鄱阳湖学刊》2016 年第 3 期。

专门有一节研究白求恩对中加文学关系的贡献。白求恩在《真正的艺术家》中说：“艺术家的作用是去打破平静。他的职责是唤醒沉睡的人们，摇撼世界上那些安于现状的栋梁。他使世界记起过去的黑暗，为世界显示当今的现实，并指出其新生之路。”[①]这是文学艺术的责任，也是侨易学的责任。

① 转引自帕特里克·墨菲著、张华译《作为自然之部分的人》，载《鄱阳湖学刊》2016年第3期。